MOUNTAIN RUNAWAYS

MOUNTAIN RUNAWAYS

PAM WITHERS

DUNDURN
PRESS

Publisher: Scott Fraser | Acquiring editor: Kathryn Lane | Editor: Susan Fitzgerald
Cover designer: Laura Boyle
Cover image: helicopter: istock.com/kevinjeon00; mountain: istock.com/Mumemories
Printer: Marquis Book Printing Inc.

Library and Archives Canada Cataloguing in Publication

Title: Mountain runaways / Pam Withers.
Names: Withers, Pam, author.
Identifiers: Canadiana (print) 20210150394 | Canadiana (ebook) 20210150408 | ISBN 9781459748316 (softcover) | ISBN 9781459748323 (PDF) | ISBN 9781459748330 (EPUB)
Classification: LCC PS8595.I8453 M68 2022 | DDC jC813/.6—dc23

We acknowledge the support of the Canada Council for the Arts and the Ontario Arts Council for our publishing program. We also acknowledge the financial support of the Government of Ontario, through the Ontario Book Publishing Tax Credit and Ontario Creates, and the Government of Canada.

Care has been taken to trace the ownership of copyright material used in this book. The author and the publisher welcome any information enabling them to rectify any references or credits in subsequent editions.

The publisher is not responsible for websites or their content unless they are owned by the publisher.

Printed and bound in Canada.

Dundurn Press
1382 Queen Street East
Toronto, Ontario, Canada M4L 1C9
dundurn.com, @dundurnpress 🐦 f 📷

ONE

Edge of Willmore Wilderness Park in west-central Alberta, Canada

It's the family's last day together, but nobody knows that yet. Nobody knows anything except that they're all tired after a full day of February snowshoeing on the mountain above their log house, and that the mist is floating down, wrapping all five in a shroud. They can't even see their tiny mountain town of Peakton below.

Jon's snowshoes crunch to a stop as he squints through the blanket of white. His father's face, ruddy as his wool scarf, turns to Jon and his siblings, Korka and Aron.

"So, kids, what do we do when visibility is bad?" Dad asks.

"Stay put," Jon says with full confidence. As if he even needs to be asked. At seventeen, he knows more than most of the adults who file through his parents' two-week wilderness-survival courses. "Or —"

"— use a compass if there's still a sightline left," his younger sister, Korka, finishes for him, flipping her thick blond braid back with gloved fingers, her blue eyes sparkling. At fourteen, she annoys Jon with her constant attempts to prove herself.

The two watch Aron plop down in the snow with the angelic smile of an eleven-year-old. It's his way of saying that when you're fogged in, you should stay where you are. And who cares about weather, anyway? If you're with the only four people who matter to you in the world, all is well.

"Good, kids," their mother, bundled in a parka, says in her enthusiastic teacher's voice. "And why do we not just continue to march forward?"

"Because without a compass —" Jon begins.

"— we'll end up going in a circle without meaning to," Korka finishes.

Aron rolls onto his back and kicks one leg up in the air like a baby moose trying to right itself, chuckling as his snowshoes send white stuff flying.

Their mom interprets: "Because we all have one leg slightly longer than the other, which means no matter how hard we try, we can't walk in a straight line without a sightline or compass." She leans down to tickle Aron through his padded snow vest. "Good answer, my young Viking."

Jon watches Aron wrap his mittens around her ankles and tug her off-balance, sending her into the snow beside him. She screeches with laughter, and they create synchronized mother-and-son snow angels. Warmth radiates through Jon's chest. It's always good watching Aron come out of his shell.

"We have a compass," Korka declares, folding her arms and frowning at her dad like she's keen to get home.

She's always got places to go, things to do, Jon reflects. Fog's not about to slow her down.

Jon, on the other hand, is happy to linger in the soup. Not only does he love an outdoor navigation challenge, but up here, there's no phone reception. That means he doesn't have to listen to whiny apologies from his date from hell at the Valentine's Day dance the previous evening. Maybe today's fog can obliterate the recurring flashback of the high school gymnasium strewn with crepe paper and the echo of her harsh words as she dumped him, shouting over the racket of a musically challenged band.

All he'd suggested was ditching the dance and going to the local café for a bite. Okay, maybe he put it too strongly. He'd felt so claustrophobic in the overwarm, overlit, jarringly noisy gym that he insisted they get out of there. She seemed to take it the wrong way, like girls always do.

"No way. We came to dance. Stop ordering me around. Like you did last week when you dragged me up a slope on a stupid, freezing 'walk.' We're done. Go find a girl who likes a bossy tyrant." After another fifteen minutes of arguing, she stalked off.

When he looked for her to apologize, he found her in a dark corner making out with some other guy.

So, being wrapped in a heavy cloud pretty much suits his mood. Besides, the last thing he wants is to get home and be yanked into his father's home office. "You're the oldest, and the most responsible, the one with a good head for marketing and numbers," his dad likes to say. "We need you to help run the survival school as soon as you graduate."

In a few months he'll march across the stage at Peakton High School. But for now, he's hopelessly clinging to his own plan for the future. He knows his parents can't afford to send him to college, but they only shake their heads when he begs them to let him get his emergency medical technician — EMT — certification this summer, a course he's been studying for every minute of his spare time. An EMT job could earn him decent money, and he'd be able to save lives in the great outdoors that he loves so much.

"Sorry, Jon," his dad has said a million times, frowning. "The survival school needs you, immediately. More work, less play when you graduate, son. It's all about earning enough to feed the family."

Jon sighs. *The family.* A family enveloped in fog at the moment and, unknown to his younger siblings, in debt.

"Let's turn around already!" Korka demands. "I want to get home in time for my Krav Maga session!"

"Hmm, not till you demonstrate something you've learned from that martial arts class," Dad says with a smile.

"It's not technically martial arts, Dad. It's a tactical defence system," she declares with her usual pout.

4

Jon rolls his eyes.

"Okay," Dad says, grinning and raising protective arms in front of his face.

The words are barely out of his mouth when Korka thumps him on the back of his neck with the palm of her hand. Not enough to hurt him, but enough to surprise him. He drops his tall, lanky frame overdramatically into the snow, playing along.

"See how I kept my elbow in front of my ribs, rather than let you expect the blow by pulling my arm back?" she asks proudly. "So you couldn't see it coming!"

Dad rubs his neck and grins. "Got that right," he says.

Laughter filters through the gauzy air between them. Then Dad leaps back up and faces her with his head lowered. Jon barely hears his next words. "I'm sorry you'll have to miss the summer sessions. We just can't afford them anymore."

She pulls away and crosses her arms. "Maybe I can ask Mrs. Alpern if I can pay for them by cleaning her basement studio every day."

"We'll talk about it later," Dad says, patting her arm.

Really? Jon thinks. *We have to mention money stuff even up here?* Still, his father has found a chance to get out of his office to spend some family time outdoors. Which is good but kind of sad, considering his business *is* being outdoors and teaching its mysteries to others. The family's survival school has been low on customers and cash for a while. Barely surviving (okay, that wasn't funny). *Mostly because Mom and Dad are better at teaching what they love than at the business end,* Jon figures.

Korka helps Aron leap up and dust off the snow, then wraps him in a warm hug that brings out a wide grin. The kind of high-beam smile that Aron gets when reading his books on Viking heroes.

"Okay," says Dad. "I say we escort Korka home to get ready for her lesson as soon as the three of you demonstrate your snow-pit competence, which will assure us that all is safe for a return using our compasses."

"Compasses are no good now that we've lost our sightline," Korka says, nose scrunched up like she's caught him out on a trick question.

"According to our last sightline a few minutes ago, home is one hundred forty degrees southeast of where we stand right now," Jon says quickly, proudly.

"Exactly, son. Well done. So, we use our compass."

None of them wants to do a snow pit, Jon figures, but they know their parents too well to bother protesting. Obediently, they drop to their knees and, using their hands and small shovels, start shovelling snow on the slope to the side of their path. The idea is to check the stability of the snowpack. It's like digging a little hole a ski-length wide and knees-to-head height, then slicing off a side like it's a piece of layer cake in need of inspection. Like preparing to poke fingers into the icing and cake layers to see if any part is so doughy or slippery that one layer might slide off another.

Within minutes, there are three side-by-side mini-pits. The siblings compete to finish, brushing their mittens vertically across the face of the pits, checking which layers are crusty and weak enough to crumble and which are hard enough that their fingers, fists, a pencil, and maybe even a knife won't go through.

"Aron, you're not digging a hole to China," Mom says.

"Nope. He's digging to Iceland," Jon says, making Aron smile. His Viking-obsessed little brother would definitely prefer to dig a hole to one of the Nordic countries.

Jon glances at Korka. She's crawling around in her tiny pit, shoving her arms into the weak layers.

Aron is smelling his, and chewing thoughtfully on some of the snow. Aron likes to do things a little differently. But when it comes down to instincts, Jon would pretty much trust his little brother with his life.

Once the pit walls are smooth and vertical, the three get to their feet, dust themselves off, and reach for the ice saw on the end of Dad's ski pole. Korka gets her hands on it first. She conducts her stability tests, then hands it to Jon.

"It's all good," she says, hands on her hips.

Jon chops out a study block roughly fingers-to-elbow length and places Dad's shovel on top of the column. Then he taps the top of the shovel, first lightly, then harder, till his cube fractures.

"Compression test hard, which is good," he rules. "Low danger." Unlike his siblings, he has had a full avalanche-training course.

An impatient Aron grabs the shovel from Jon, completes his test, and offers a thumbs-up. He *can* speak — he just prefers not to. That's how it's been ever since the three siblings had a childhood misadventure that their parents never found out about, and that Jon figures the other two were too young to remember. It's a trauma he wishes he could forget, too.

"You're all correct. Low avalanche danger between here and home," Dad confirms.

A nearby crunch of snow startles them. Two large, shadowy figures on cross-country skis emerge from the mist.

"Ha!" bellows Officer Greg Vine, the absolute last person Jon wants to see right now. He's the cop father of the girl he took out last night.

Greg's brother, David, equally big and muscle-bound as his brother, pauses behind him.

"Got your kids on their knees praying for the mist to blow away, Gunnar and Eva?" Officer Vine asks. "Is that a strange Icelandic tradition? Or is this snow-pit school?"

As if we need schooling on snow pits, which we've been making all our lives, Jon thinks.

"They're practising their snow pits, Greg," Dad replies breezily. "Remember, kids, always dig them on a slope that's the same aspect and angle as the slope you're about to travel across, without triggering an avalanche."

"We know that, Dad," Jon says.

"Of course you do." He grins and turns back to the men. "Are we on for skiing first thing tomorrow morning, gentlemen?"

"Storm coming in, so it depends on conditions," Officer Vine replies, his dark eyes on Jon. As Jon's mother and father move ahead out of earshot, the big cop says in a low voice, "Jon Gunnarsson. When you pick my daughter up for a date, I expect you to deliver her home, not ditch her at the dance and make her walk home in the dark."

Korka, who was at the dance, overhears and smirks. Aron scrunches up his face at Officer Vine's back. It occurs to Jon that Aron did the same to his recent date's back. Guess he should've taken note.

"She ditched me," Jon says, hardly believing he has the guts to stand up to the town's entire police force — all two of them. He looks at the hulking, hard-faced men. "I don't suppose she told you that."

"I don't care about your squabbles. I care about my daughter's safety. And about your level of responsibility, young man. I forbid you from seeing her again, Jon. End of story." Officer Vine skis ahead to catch up with Jon's parents. "See you tomorrow, Gunnar," he says in a much lighter tone. "Good day, Eva."

Jon glances back long enough to nod at Korka and stare overlong at Aron. It reminds him of the time Officer Vine said to Greg, when he thought no one else could hear him, "I admire them for trying to raise that kid themselves, but between you and me, I think he might do better in a special home with experts on autism and muteness."

Aron is *not* mute. He speaks sometimes, but mostly only around family members. Nor is he a high-functioning autistic person, as one specialist ruled.

"Clearly a misdiagnosis from someone who never sees him interact at home," their mother declared of the specialist. "He's just ... Aron."

Exactly. Jon figures Aron could beat Officer Vine at any intelligence test. Plus, his kid brother has a remarkable ability to instantly suss out people and situations. Korka calls him their family psychic. The kid just knows stuff, sometimes for no good reason. Like (as he's said) that Officer Vine is jealous of the Gunnarsson family's outdoor skills, and that he's a mean, two-faced guy.

The two cops swish down the trail like awkward gorillas on skis.

"Everyone good for the final leg home?" their dad asks.

"We're all good," Jon says, yanking his wool hat down almost over his eyes.

"Let's go already," Korka adds.

Aron agrees with a thumbs-up.

TWO

"Dump her. She's not your type. And you don't have to take that kind of crap from any girl."

Jon is lazing in bed the next morning, on the phone with his best buddy, Mark. It's Mark's sympathy, not what he's saying, that Jon needs right now. Jon can ace anything that has to do with outdoor survival — danger is what makes him feel alive — but girls? He flunks that subject regularly.

"Take them out on real dates," his pushy sister likes to say. "Don't make them do only what you want to do. Girls don't like control-freak guys whose idea of romance is making a snow cave. Or feeding them freeze-dried chili cooked on a camp stove and expecting them to sleep in a mouldy tent."

"Her dad had the nerve to chew me out for not walking her home," Jon tells Mark.

"Officer Vine can be a jerk. Hence his daughter's personality. I say stay well clear of 'em both."

"Must be cold out," Jon says, changing the subject. "My bedroom window is totally frosted up."

"Yeah, howling wind and snow all night last night," Mark says. "Would've been epic to be out in that."

It's why the two are so tight. They live to test themselves out in the wild. Like the time they snuck out of their houses during a snowstorm, dragged hammocks from their storage space in the Gunnarsson garage, and hung them from trees in the backyard. They tried sleeping in the hammocks with only emergency blankets wrapped around them. Two hours later, they snuck back inside with damp, droopy pyjamas, undetected by Jon's parents and thrilled to have survived, though both came down with colds that kept them out of school for a week.

Jon rises to rub a clear circle on his window glass. "Blue sky. We could do some killer snowboarding today." Way off to the right, he sees his father digging a snow pit on their mountain. Then Jon is distracted by his mom's phone ringing downstairs. A minute later he hears her shout.

"Jon!" Mom pads up the stairs.

"Got to go, Mark," Jon says. "Talk later."

"Later." Mark clicks off.

Mom enters his bedroom in her red wool bathrobe and beaded mooseskin slippers, holding a steaming cup of coffee in one hand, her phone in the other. She perches on the edge of his bed.

"It wasn't for you, but it concerns you," she says with a tentative smile. "A couple from Rockvale wants to hire us to track down their daughter, who ran away from home a while ago." Rockvale is half an hour's drive away. "They suspect she's hiding in the woods north of here. They're offering a lot for us to find her." She takes a deep breath. "We really need the money, so if —"

"Interesting," Jon says, perking up. "How long ago? I haven't heard anything about a missing person. Did they call the police? What about Search and Rescue?"

"Leah — that's her name — is eighteen, so officially an adult in Alberta. As far as I know, they didn't file a missing-persons report. For some reason, they want to keep it private."

"So, why are they calling you?"

"She took our advanced wilderness-survival course last summer. So, I guess they think we might have some insight into where she could be hiding." Mom takes a sip of her coffee. "I'll get more info. But can Dad and I count on your help with this if we accept the job?"

"Of course."

The doorbell sounds. Mom rises and shuffles down the stairs to the entryway, still holding the phone and coffee cup.

From the upstairs landing, Jon sees Greg and David Vine step into the hallway, shaking snow off their parkas. Korka, who has stepped out of her bedroom across the hall from his, peers at them, too. The men are fully outfitted for backcountry skiing. Jon backs into his room at the same time Korka backs into hers, and he hurries to dress.

13

He hears Mom greet them. "Hi, guys. Gunnar's just testing the snow at the foot of Cinnamon Run."

"More than thirty centimetres of white stuff last night, on top of that ice crust we've had for a while," Officer Vine says, shaking his head. "Can't expect all that to bond well. I'm definitely worried about slabbing."

"A valid concern, but only on the leeward side of the mountain," booms Dad's voice as he appears behind them, stomping snow off his boots. "Just did compression tests in a couple of spots, and I called my buddy at the heli-ski lodge. If we hike up through the trees beside Cinnamon Run to Ridgeline, and ski down Nutmeg Slope on the other side, it won't be great snow, but it'll be okay. Cinnamon would be marginal today, for sure."

Jon glances out the window at Cinnamon Run, now deserted. Normally, skiers *whoosh* down its steep slope to a runout just left of their house and the handful of other buildings that make up Peakton, elevation 1,829 metres. Hemmed by trees and rock walls, this is the leeward side of the mountain, the part overshadowed by a giant cornice that resembles the curl of a frozen surf wave about to crash down on the valley.

"Okay," Officer Vine says, less than confidently. "I trust you, Gunnar. We're ready to go when you are, then. Meet you at the bottom of Evergreen Trail."

"Be there in two minutes." Dad steps into the house for his skis and pack.

"I put some freshly baked banana bread in your pack," Mom says. She touches the avalanche beacon hanging around his neck, like she always does to reassure herself it'll keep him safe. If he were ever buried in the snow, the beacon would emit a radio signal that could be picked up by his companions' transceivers so they would know where to dig him out.

Dad smiles, sets Mom's coffee cup down, and sweeps her off her feet for a Hollywood-style kiss.

"Get a room," Korka says as she skips down the stairs, Aron moving more cautiously behind her.

"Okay, you're next," Dad says, scooping Korka up and planting a loud kiss on her forehead. Then he peers up the stairs. "Jon? Bear hug for your old man?"

Jon steps onto the landing and makes his way down to give his tall, strong father a dutiful clasp.

"So proud of you, son," Dad says. "Keep an eye on your siblings today."

"Aron and I don't need bossy Big Viking keeping an eye on us," Korka pipes up.

Dad smiles and squats down to Aron's height with a questioning look. Like he wants permission to hug his favourite. As if Aron would ever refuse him. But Jon is shocked when Aron throws himself at Dad, locks his arms around his ankles, and bellows like a grizzly cub.

"Don't go!" Aron refuses to release his grip.

Mom exchanges a look with Dad, then wraps her hands around Aron's to pry him away. Jon feels shivers travel down his spine, but he isn't sure why.

"It's okay, my young Viking," Mom says softly, holding Aron firmly to her as he forms his hands into fists and beats on her stomach.

Jon's chest remains tight as Dad grabs his skis and pack and backs out the door.

"Thanks for the banana bread, honey. Love you all."

Mom and Korka have their hands full trying to calm Aron, so Jon heads back upstairs to check his phone. Fifteen minutes later, he hears Mom shout for him. This time something's wrong — she sounds frantic.

He races down to see Mom tossing off her red house-coat and slippers and pulling on a white ski suit over her thermal long underwear.

"Jon! Look after Korka and Aron. I'll be right back!" she shouts as she flies out the front door.

Aron tries to dive for her ankles, so Jon manhandles him into the living room. Korka follows, her eyebrows raised. Grabbing binoculars from the windowsill, Jon positions himself at the pane that frames Cinnamon Run. He spots Dad and his buddies stepping onto the ridge.

Mom is sprinting up Evergreen Trail. What's wrong? Did Dad forget something important?

As Aron and Korka grab for the binoculars, their father veers away from his ski mates and then, unbeliev-ably, leaps from the cornice over Cinnamon Run.

"He's going for it!" Korka announces, half-impressed, half-terrified.

After a beautiful airborne arc, Dad lands on Cinna-mon. A plume follows his smooth, skilled skiing as he cuts across the empty face. Only he would dare such a ride after a big snow dump. But that wasn't the plan! What the heck is he doing? And what's Mom doing?

Just then, the trail his father is blazing gives way, unleashing a deadly slide. Aron's and Korka's screams deafen Jon, and he clenches his fist to keep from crying out, too, as all three witness their father struggle to keep control and then disappear into the snow tsunami. Their mom stands frozen at the edge of the trees, as do the Vine brothers up top. Jon knows they're waiting for the slide to stop. And for sure the guys are busy double-checking that their avalanche beacons are on, ready to move in and find Dad if he gets buried.

Buried. A memory thrusts itself to the front of Jon's brain. He feels smothered and panicky, but pushes it away, like he did that long-ago day, to grapple with the reality of this moment.

When Aron and Korka turn toward the front door, Jon grabs them by their collars and stops them.

"He'll be all right," he assures them, though his whole body has gone stone cold. "The men have beacons. They know what they're doing." But do they? Dad once said Greg and David nearly flunked his avalanche safety course. "Stop yelling, Aron. Send positive energy instead. They'll dig him out. We'd only be in the way."

Aron struggles against Jon's firm grip as if determined to escape. Korka looks from Aron to Jon, obviously torn. But then they see Mom dart out from the trees. She stops just below where they last saw Dad.

"Nooo!" Korka screams.

"She doesn't have a beacon!" Korka hollers. "She needs one to find him!"

Aron stops wriggling and stands stock-still.

Jon's stomach lurches. Korka's right. Mom needs a beacon. But maybe Mom's so sure she knows where he is that she'll be the miracle rescuer?

All three stand frozen at the window, eyes fixed on Greg and David, who are skiing back and forth purposefully, their beacons in their hands. The siblings are well aware that the men might trigger a secondary slide. It's not a safe place for them to be. Dad would tell them so, if he were —

Fifteen minutes is all Jon can think. Most avalanche victims die from suffocation or trauma, but a buried victim can hold out for up to fifteen minutes. His toes curl tightly. He's desperate to be up there digging with the men and Mom. *I can save Dad. I know I can.*

"Sorry, sorry! Don't know what I was thinking," Dad will say as he struggles up from under the snow, face flushed with excitement. "But thanks for yanking me out, son."

Instead, Jon wraps his arms around Korka and Aron as they stand like ice sculptures in front of the window.

"Mom said she'll be right back," Korka says. "She promised."

Just then, their worst nightmare plays out in front of their eyes: The men above have triggered a smaller slide. They're just managing to ski out of its grip, but — *no!* — Mom disappears in its white cloud.

"Mom!" Aron screams and tears himself away from Jon. He has his boots on and the door open before Jon can stop him.

Jon pauses only long enough to stuff his bare feet into boots, then takes off after Aron, with Korka on his heels. As his rugged soles form one print after another in the snow, the world slows down to a blinding, noiseless white.

Jon is way faster, stronger, and bigger than Aron, and soon he's just an inch away from grabbing his brother's coatless form. Yet some force is keeping him from throwing himself on top of Aron. Does he know where she is? Jon doesn't know how many minutes have elapsed when, suddenly, Aron jumps off-trail right below where the second slide has stopped, leaps like a wild rabbit upslope, and begins digging with his bare hands.

Wordlessly, Korka and Jon follow suit. Yes! A grey furry boot. They work faster, harder, as people from the village run toward them. They uncover her torso, then her face. Her eyes are closed. Jon leans down and places his cheek above her lips, his finger on the side of her neck to feel for a pulse.

No breath, no pulse. "Don't leave us, don't leave us," he moans. He places his hands above her waist and sets them exactly where she herself taught him, to perform cardiopulmonary resuscitation. He begins the life-saving moves with a focus that pushes the rest of the world away.

One-and-two-and-three-and … Thirty chest compressions, two rescue breaths.

"Son, I'm an EMT," says a man standing over Jon, someone Jon knows. "Good work. I'll take over now. Get yourself and those kids out of here. It's too unstable."

Jon ignores him. *One-and-two-and-three-and —*

"Jon!" Korka is pulling on him. "Stop Aron!"

Jon blinks and looks up, and the EMT steps in seamlessly. Sure enough, Aron is darting uphill to where the search continues for Dad. Right into the avalanche's deadly trigger zone, the place it's most likely to let loose again.

This time Jon tackles his hell-bent brother in microseconds and carries him, kicking and screaming, back down the slope. He hesitates as he passes the medics working on Mom, fear clogging his throat and paralyzing his feet. It takes all his willpower to walk by her still form, but he knows for sure his brother and sister have seen enough. He leaves the avalanche zone, his squirming brother still slung over his shoulder.

"Korka! Follow me! I need your help with Aron!" he commands, heading for the house. She moves mechanically after him.

It's up to him to protect his brother and sister, hide them from the crowds forming, the noise and red lights of the arriving ambulance, the shouting, the looks. No matter what happens, the three of them need to be alone and together right now. Shaken as he is, he needs to be the strong one.

Back in the house, they sink into the living room sofa, Jon's hand still locked on Aron's arm. They stare blank-eyed out the living room window. Aron covers his ears against the ambulance's wail.

Any minute now, Jon tells himself, Mom will be helped inside, cold and shaken but otherwise fine, and announce that Dad has been dug out and all is well. Eventually, a paramedic will arrive to offer them a ride to the hospital to visit their dad in recovery. Jon's counting on it. The front door's unlocked, waiting for someone in authority to open it, walk through, and give them good news.

But the door doesn't move, and they stare at it as the air seems to grow icier, creeping around them, chilling them to the bone.

THREE

Korka, seated on the living room sofa, watches Jon lower the living room blinds and flick on some lights. Even so, afternoon shadows seem to reach in and darken the house's interior. She holds her body dead still. It feels shattered, useless. Her big brother has the phone in his hand, and it vibrates constantly, but he just stares at it. She makes no attempt to grab it or point out that someone's calling.

When the doorbell rings, all three kids jump.

Aron sprints to it. Seeing Officer Vine and the woman who is their family doctor standing there solemnly, Aron screams and slams it shut in their faces. Then he locks it and races upstairs.

Korka sighs. Her chest feels hollow. Breathing seems hard work. Tears squeeze out from under her eyelids, despite an urgent battle to stop them. Finally, she surrenders and melts into a bawling wreck, clinging to Jon's chest. In war movies, it's always two uniformed officers who appear at the widow's door, carrying a folded flag in their hands. This is not a movie.

"Don't let them in," Korka pleads. "Don't unlock the door. Wait for Mom and Dad to get home."

"I have to, Korka," Jon says quietly, easing her off him gently. "Go upstairs to be with Aron if you want."

As he rises slowly to his feet, she flops herself face down on the sofa. The front door is made of solid cedar panels, designed and constructed by Dad. Last summer Korka helped him varnish and glue-gun the panels into place. She remembers watching him and Jon lift the door into the hinged frame. At the time, it opened onto dewy green grass, purple flowers, and birdsong. The door is a work of art, but it is heavy. She watches Jon struggle to open it like he's wrestling the north wind itself.

Officer Vine and the doctor are still standing there wordlessly, measuring the two of them with a sympathy she can't bear.

"You know Dr. Lindsay, right?" Officer Vine begins in a low, controlled voice. "May we come in?" He hasn't had time to change into his police uniform for this official duty.

Dr. Lindsay walks directly to the sofa to place an arm on Korka, who forces herself to sit up. The doctor directs a sad face at her as Officer Vine closes the door softly.

Korka opens her mouth, but her throat is too tight for anything to come out. Jon backs halfway into the living room, bumps into the sofa, and falls onto it beside her. Unable to stop herself, Korka leaps up in a surge of anger, half intending to take a run at Officer Vine. Then she collapses in a heap on the floor, her head down for a moment, tangled yellow hair spilling over her face, fists still bunched up. What's Officer Vine doing here? She doesn't want to hear anything he has to say.

Their long-time doctor has an almost frightened look on her face. It vaguely occurs to Korka that she doesn't want to be here any more than they want her here.

"Sit down, Jon. And Korka," Officer Vine says firmly. "Where's Aron?"

"Upstairs, hiding," Jon replies.

Officer Vine nods at Dr. Lindsay, who hesitates, then climbs the stairs. She returns minutes later. "He's under a bed," she reports quietly. "I think it's okay to leave him there for the moment. Korka, do you mind letting us speak with Jon alone?"

"I'm not moving," Korka says, her voice breaking, her hands over her face.

"Anything you say to me, you can say to her," Jon says. "If she doesn't want to leave, you can't make her, anyway."

Filled with gratitude, Korka bites her tongue and sits up on the carpet. Jon pushes himself into the sofa back as the adults take seats in two tattered armchairs across from them. The only sounds in the house are the ticking grandfather clock and Aron's moans from upstairs.

"Against protocol," Officer Vine says.

"Let her stay," Dr. Lindsay rules.

When no one else replies, Officer Vine asks, "How old are you, Jon?"

"Seventeen."

"Yes, but when do you come of age?"

"I turn eighteen in less than three months," he says. His words come out like a hoarse bark.

It figures he gets all the questions, Korka thinks. Like she's not even there.

"I see. Who's your next of kin?"

"We have none."

"We'll be double-checking that, of course," Officer Vine says as he scribbles in a notepad. "But if that's the case, it means you need a guardian or guardians until then. You'll receive a visit from Children's Services shortly. That's the government ministry that will oversee your care. Meanwhile, my wife will come over and stay with you. She'll be here any moment."

"No, thanks," Jon says sharply.

"No, thanks," Korka echoes, proud of her brother's courage. This is not happening, *not happening.* Korka gnaws on her lip. *Mom, Dad, what are we supposed to do?*

"Why do you need to know about next of kin?" Jon asks. "Where are our parents? Are they okay?" Korka hears panic rising in his voice.

"I'm sorry to tell you that both of your parents have died," Officer Vine continues, looking at this notepad like he's reading from a script.

"No!" Korka screams. Her head jerks up, her body electrified in horror. Dr. Lindsay holds out a hand to her, but Korka ignores it. "They teach *survival*! They know *everything*! Nothing can kill them. We got to Mom in time, and Dad ... Dad has a beacon!" Don't they know it's impossible that Mom and Dad are dead?

Officer Vine holds up his hand, and Korka goes silent. Jon's breathing has gone uneven, like he's struggling to catch his breath. He reaches out to Korka and pulls her onto the sofa beside him. She buries her head in his neck, speechless and numb.

"Both died of asphyxiation." The officer delivers the devastating words slowly and carefully. "Your father's beacon had faulty batteries. We required rescue dogs to find his body." He pauses. "We temporarily revived your mother, but I'm sorry to tell you she died in the ambulance on the way to the hospital."

"No!" Jon shouts, pounding a fist into the sofa arm, sending up a plume of dust. "That's impossible! We got to her right away!"

Korka chokes back a scream. There is silence for a moment. Then the moaning upstairs starts again, louder now. Dr. Lindsay looks at the stairs, then at Officer Vine.

"Do we leave it to you to tell Aron?" Officer Vine asks. "The challenged kid," he says as an aside to Dr. Lindsay, who winces at his using that phrase in front of the siblings.

As if the doctor hasn't known Aron all his life, doesn't understand his quirkiness way better than Officer Vine ever will. Korka would love to deliver a Krav Maga chop to the officer's neck.

"Leave Aron alone," Jon warns, eyes narrowing on Officer Vine, heat rushing to his face. Korka hides her face in Jon's shirt, her tears soaking it. Her body has gone limp. She refuses to look at their visitors.

"I'm sorry, Jon, but I need to try," Dr. Lindsay says gently, and she starts up the stairs.

"The hospital needs you to identify your parents," Officer Vine says to Jon, his voice low. "The coroner will be doing an autopsy, and the hospital needs to know soon whether you want the bodies sent to a —"

"Stop!" Dr. Lindsay calls from the landing in a furious voice.

Korka raises her head. Officer Vine's face is turning red. He doesn't finish the sentence.

What feels like a fist inside Korka's throat stops her from saying anything. Jon, who has fallen mute, seems to be suffering the same thing.

"I can drive you to the hospital now to see them, if you want."

Korka joins Jon in just staring at the police officer. *He did not just say that. I'm going to attack him for real if he says it again.*

"Do either of you have any questions?" Dr. Lindsay asks sadly as she descends the stairs, apparently not so set on talking to Aron. She sits back down in the armchair.

"Yes." Jon turns to Officer Vine accusingly. "Why didn't you stick to your plan of doing Nutmeg? Why did Dad start down Cinnamon?"

Korka shoots hate-dart eyes at Officer Vine while waiting for his answer.

The large man sighs and stares at his hands. "We had no intention of doing Cinnamon. But as we got on the ridge, Gunnar shouted, 'This line looks amazing! I'm really feeling it!' And he jumped off onto it. Jon, Korka, your father was my favourite ski mate and the most skilled backcountry man I've ever had the privilege of knowing. He could be impulsive and he liked taking risks, but I will never understand — we will never understand — why he deviated from the plan and leapt onto Cinnamon like that." Officer Vine rubs his face with his hands.

After a moment, he continues. "David and I tried, son, really tried, to reach him in time. I believe we would have if his beacon's batteries had been working. But can you explain why your mother followed him?"

Korka flashes back to how Mom's face lost colour when Aron tried to stop Dad from leaving. She's sure Mom sensed that Aron had had a premonition of some sort. It took Mom a while to act on it, but Korka's not about to say that.

"Obviously he doesn't know!" Dr. Lindsay objects. She turns to Jon and Korka. "We'll stay with you till Mrs. Vine gets here. I should warn you, too, that there are newspaper and TV reporters gathering outside."

"Reporters?" Jon chokes on the word.

"Why?" Korka adds, rubbing her damp face with her sleeve.

"What has happened is, unfortunately, news," Officer Vine says quietly.

Korka takes a deep breath, feeling like a cornice is collapsing beneath her.

"Thank you," Jon says.

Thank you? For not rescuing our father, and then showing up here to —

"You're welcome," the two adults say together, shifting in their seats.

The doorbell sounds. Officer Vine's face relaxes. "That'll be my wife. She'll stay with you tonight," he says in the careful monotone that's starting to enrage Korka.

No! she wants to say. *Get out of our house now! This is not real!*

Officer Vine opens the door. Mrs. Vine, a skinny, hesitant woman, accepts her husband's peck on the cheek, steps in, and fumbles with her coat.

"I'm … I'm so, so sorry for your loss," she says, twisting her hands. She stops when her husband gives her a look. "Um, where's Aron?"

"Upstairs. Let them go to him," Dr. Lindsay says. "Jon, Korka, are you okay with us going now, or do you want us to stay longer? I've put our phone numbers here on the table in case you have any questions."

"We're okay," Jon manages to say.

Korka figures it's the biggest lie he has ever uttered.

"I'm sorry," the doctor says in a genuine tone. A tear escapes her eye as she places one hand on Jon's shoulder and the other on Korka's.

"Thank you," Jon manages. Korka squeezes her eyelids shut. As Jon strokes her hair, Korka counts to ten, hoping all the adults but Mrs. Vine will be gone when she opens her eyes. She opens them a microsecond too soon, just in time to see, through the open door, a couple of strangers with television cameras and microphones parked in their front yard. The reporters throng Officer Vine and Dr. Lindsay when they step outside. As Dr. Lindsay shuts the door firmly behind her, Korka rises and dodges Mrs. Vine to double-bolt it.

"What can I do?" Mrs. Vine asks, standing awkwardly beside the coat hooks, her hands clasped in front of her. "Would you like something to drink or eat?"

"Make coffee for yourself?" Jon suggests. "And please, just give us space."

She nods apologetically. As soon as she has disappeared into the kitchen, Jon turns to Korka.

"We need to pull down all the shades in the house and check on Aron," he says, his voice hoarse. She nods and helps him with the window coverings.

Aron needs Mom, but he will respond to me, Korka tells herself. *I need to act brave for him.*

"We need time alone upstairs," Jon calls out to Mrs. Vine. She comes to the kitchen doorway and nods, eyes flitting to piles of laundry and discarded dishes in the living room.

Aron is not in his room, nor in Korka's or Jon's. Korka's heart skips a beat. Then she notices that Mom and Dad's bed is missing its sky-blue duvet and pillows. She finds Aron wrapped in the duvet under their parents' bed, whimpering.

Despite Jon's size, he manages to squeeze under the bed, the slats scraping his back. Korka slithers in from the other side. The two wrap their arms around Aron, but this turns him into a fighter.

"We're smothering him. Give him some space," Korka whispers to Jon. Aron is claustrophobic, scared of small, dark spaces, and they are blocking him in. Korka rearranges herself so that Aron's face is to the light, then wraps her little brother in her arms and puts his moist face firmly against her own. The boy stills. Korka can feel Jon's breath from the other side of Aron's neck.

"Did you hear?" Korka whispers.

Aron nods.

They're all crying now, amid the dustballs and the scent of Mom and Dad in the bedclothes wrapped around Aron, which he eventually holds out to share with them. Clinging to one another in a tangle of limbs, the three stay for hours in the half dark beneath the bed slats, oblivious to the phone and doorbell ringing.

Once, Korka hears Mrs. Vine climb the stairs, sees the red leather shoes pause near her face, and closes her eyes as the woman leans down to peer at them. She's relieved when the unwanted caretaker says nothing, just backs off and pads down the stairs again.

Eventually, Jon and Korka wriggle out, tug their little brother clear, and lift his sleeping form into Mom and Dad's bed. Then they tread softly downstairs. Jon exchanges a few words with Mrs. Vine. Korka avoids her attempt at a hug.

"I know you may not want me here," Mrs. Vine says in her kind but nervous voice, "but no one in the community will accept your being alone right now. So, let me help where I can, okay, Jon?"

Like Korka's not there.

"Okay," Korka hears Jon say with a sigh. But it's true they don't want her here, and they don't feel like making conversation. They traipse back up the stairs like sleep-walkers and sit like zombies on either side of sleeping Aron. Korka looks at her big brother, who is staring at his phone.

"Full of messages," he mumbles before turning it off.

She lies down and is almost asleep when she hears the doorbell, then a very loud, hard-to-ignore knock on the door.

She and Jon both leap up. From the stair landing, they watch a panicked Mrs. Vine peering out the blinds.

"Don't open it," Jon shouts down to her.

But even from the staircase, Korka can hear a woman's voice. "I'm with Children's Services. Please let me in. You are required to by law."

FOUR

Jon trudges down the stairs, not wanting to greet anyone but knowing Mrs. Vine will open the door if he doesn't. Korka nearly knocks him over as she scurries past him to confront the visitor, defence moves at the ready. So touchy, but that's Korka.

Mrs. Vine opens the door before either of them reaches it. Jon watches a woman squeeze her slim form through the door as if determined not to let the photographers get a shot of them, a photo that would probably run with a caption like *Tragic avalanche victims' orphans* in the next day's paper.

"Hello," the lady says, as Mrs. Vine closes and locks the door behind her. "Mrs. Vine? I'm Amanda Pierce from Children's Services." She turns to Jon and Korka. "Jon and Korka, I presume? I'm very sorry for your loss." The words sound more heartfelt coming from her than they did from Officer Vine.

"Hi," Jon says tiredly.

Korka squints at their visitor and moves back toward the sofa. "Why'd you let her in?" she asks Mrs. Vine.

"I had to, honey," Mrs. Vine says.

Korka scowls. Nobody calls Korka *honey* and gets away with it, Jon muses.

"Against the law not to," he explains to his sister. "And she's trying to help us."

Amanda shoots Jon an appreciative look.

She has a pleasant face, long black hair, a purple parka that matches her rugged nylon briefcase, and grey furry boots identical to Mom's. She sheds those just inside the door, right beside where Mom's usually are. Mrs. Vine takes her coat.

This social worker is barely out of college, Jon decides.

"Welcome, Amanda," Mrs. Vine says. "Would you like some coffee and cookies?"

"Actually, Mrs. Vine," Jon says as politely as he can, "would you mind leaving while Amanda, Korka, and I talk?" Maybe he shouldn't call the social worker by her first name, but it's too late now.

Although her eyes widen, Mrs. Vine is quick to reply. "Of course, Jon. If that's what you'd like. I'll slip back home till you're finished." She pulls on her gear and steps out the front door. Her place is only a few houses away.

Jon motions Amanda to an easy chair, and he and Korka sit on the sofa.

Amanda tugs a pencil and file folder out of her brief-case. "Jon, age seventeen. Korka, age fourteen, and Aron, age eleven, correct?"

"Yes. Aron is upstairs sleeping," Jon informs her.

"Jon, your birthday is May eighth, am I right? When you turn eighteen?"

"Yes."

"So, unfortunately, that means you are wards of the state until we can establish legal guardians for you. Who is your next of kin?" She looks from Jon to Korka.

Korka speaks up. "Um, we don't have any relatives. Both our parents are only children. Mom's parents died in a boat-ing accident when she was nineteen. Dad's mother died when he was young, and his father passed away last year."

"I see."

Korka continues. "Mom and Dad grew up in Iceland, eloped when they were twenty, and moved here." Jon throws an annoyed look at her.

Amanda nods. "Any other living relatives?" she asks in a kind voice.

"No. It's just the three of us," Jon says.

"I see. Well, do you have a close family friend, an adult?" She looks toward the front door meaningfully.

"No," Jon answers before Korka can.

The Vines and their parents are neighbours and ski mates, but there's no way they are good friends. Mostly, their parents hung out with survival-school staff. Staff that came and went like they were going through a revolving door. He wonders if he should mention his friend Mark, then remembers that Mark has five younger brothers and sisters, all stuffed into a tiny, drafty house.

"Our parents have friends," Jon says, refusing to use the past tense, "but no one who ... anyway, I can take care of Korka and Aron. We don't need anyone!"

"Yeah, we don't need anyone." Korka sits up, spine very straight. Jon relaxes slightly.

Amanda looks at them with a warm smile, which, for a split second, Jon soaks in like someone suffering from lack of sun.

"Of course you can, but according to the law, you need a legal guardian until Jon comes of age. There are big decisions to make over the next weeks and months. Like planning a funeral, getting your parents' will probated —"

"Pro-whatted?" Jon asks, feeling his face lose colour. He blocks out the word *funeral* with all the self-control he can muster.

"The wishes in their will followed through by an executor, death certificates, and lots more."

Jon gulps. "Can you help us with that stuff?"

The social worker's eyes are kind, but her mechanical pencil taps the folder. "Are you aware that Officer Vine and his wife have offered to be your legal guardians while these things are sorted out, and until you turn of legal age? He's taking up a collection from people in the community to pay for the funeral. He himself has pledged twenty-five hundred dollars. And they have presented themselves to us as your parents' friends."

"Just neighbours!" Korka shouts.

Jon merely stares at the social worker.

Amanda's tone goes soft. "Do you have another candidate to suggest? Or an objection to the Vines?"

"Yes! He's an asshole and my ex-girlfriend's father," Jon says, making Korka break into a fleeting smile.

"And our brother Aron hates him!" Korka adds for good measure.

The lady nods and eyes the two of them sympathetically, but not sympathetically enough for Jon.

"Did he say he'd put Aron in a home?" Jon demands.

Amanda looks startled. "I'm not at liberty —"

"Yes, you are, and he did, then," Jon says, so fiercely that Amanda gives a curt nod, then studies her notes with lowered eyes.

"He mentioned that he'd be willing to help Aron and his special needs."

Jon jumps to his feet and shouts, "You mean help break up our family!" Anger is good. It keeps a flood of hurt and sadness from overwhelming him.

He catches Korka throwing the social worker an evil look to show her they're in agreement on that one.

"I can leave you a brochure, and come back tomorrow when you've had time to think about things," Amanda says. "Jon, Officer Vine will pick you up soon for a visit to … to identify your parents."

Jon shudders but keeps his face expressionless for Korka.

"I understand why you might not be answering the phone, but I would appreciate your responding to my calls, even if you're not answering anyone else's at this point. Please know that you can call me at any time, with any question. I'm here for you. This is my direct number."

She rises, hands Jon a brochure and card, and slides the folder into her briefcase. Korka grabs the brochure from Jon's hands. "Steps to Take after a Loved One Dies," she reads, then tosses it to the floor like it could bite.

Jon retrieves it, to be polite, and walks behind Amanda as she heads for the door. The social worker is texting someone, presumably Mrs. Vine. Crazy as it sounds, he doesn't want this lady to leave right now. He wants to invite her to stay for coffee, like his mom would have. More than that, he wants to beg her to turn their world right side up again. He wants her to make the reporters go away. He wants to see if Aron scrunches up his nose at Amanda's back, and he wants her to be the guardian they have to have, but don't need. Is it because he is half-crazed at the moment? Maybe it's 'cause he hasn't even started to ask himself the questions that go with being part of a family struck twice by lightning just hours before. Is it because Amanda has the same boots as Mom? Good, sturdy grey ones.

"Do you hike?" Jon asks Amanda, for no logical reason.

"Yes, quite a lot," she replies, head cocked in mild surprise. "Usually with my brother, who works for Search and Rescue over in Wolfsburg. I understand you're quite an outdoorsman yourself."

"Me, too," Korka insists, smiling and pushing in front of Jon.

"Of course you are," Amanda says gently. Then, more firmly, "Tomorrow, I'll bring the guardianship papers to sign, designating Mr. and Mrs. Vine. Unless you call me with another name."

Jon and Korka exchange looks. "Thank you," they manage to mumble as their visitor slips her small feet into her furry boots. She squeezes her body back through the barely open door to prevent reporters from glimpsing their stunned, needy faces.

A minute later, Mrs. Vine lets herself back in through the same slot. "Amanda texted me that she was leaving," she explains. "Can I fetch you food? Do you need help with Aron? And it's okay if I sleep here in the living room? I know where your mother keeps the spare sheets, and I brought my own towel and facecloth."

"Okay," Jon says. "I'll help you with the futon."

"Thank you, Jon." She places her hand on his shoulder, and this time he doesn't mind.

The knocking and doorbell ringing start after that, men and women calling out media credentials through the door. Mrs. Vine is good about ignoring them, her jaw set.

"Leave us alone!" Korka hollers through the thick cedar panel. Then, turning to Jon with a pained face, she asks, "Is there anything to eat?"

Mrs. Vine leaps up as if relieved to have something to do. As she finds a can of baked beans and a loaf of bread in the cupboard, thoughts pummel Jon. If they don't move in with the Vines, where will he find money for groceries when they run out? How long can they hide out in their house before reporters get bored and leave? How long before their landlord throws them out for lack of rent? But the scariest thought of all: How can he stop Officer Vine from tearing them apart?

Only yesterday he was annoyed that his parents wanted him to work straight after high school and pissed at being insulted and deserted by his date — who he's now supposed to live under the same roof with? Arghh! He clings desperately to the notion he'll wake up in a moment and this will all be just a terrible nightmare. His worst one ever.

Despite being kids of survival instructors, the trio is totally unprepared to survive what's coming at them. Jon doesn't know how to clamp down on Korka's temper and snarkiness or how to comfort Aron. Nor will Mrs. Vine. He knows nothing about wills or insurance or credit cards. Only that Mom and Dad had been worrying a lot about money lately. And how are they supposed to organize or pay for a funeral if it's more than the twenty-five hundred dollars the Vines have offered?

"I can help," someone is saying. It's Korka, holding out the can opener and a saucepan.

And that's when Officer Vine arrives. "Time to go to the morgue, son," he says.

FIVE

An hour later, Korka and Aron are seated between Mom's and Dad's pillows on their bed. Korka is coaxing Aron, who sits silent and dazed-looking, to eat some warmed-up beans on toast.

Jon peeks around the worn window shade to see reporters still camped out in their front yard. Then he joins his siblings for a few forkfuls of beans, though he feels little hunger after doing his duty at the morgue. He stares at the nearest wall to banish all other thoughts.

Mrs. Vine is dusting and vacuuming the living room downstairs. She has checked on Aron only once, then backed out of the room without even saying anything to him, clearly as uncomfortable around their little brother as her husband is.

"It's not a big deal. Some people are just like that. They can't help it," their mom used to say of the Vines.

"No way we're living with the Vines," Jon says quietly, "and no way we're letting them put us in different places. Even if it was for a short while, we might not get you back easily, Aron."

"Agreed," Korka says with a sigh.

Aron tells them his vote by resting his hands on both their arms.

"But who else could be our guardian?" Korka asks.

Jon and Korka go through the names of other friends' parents and their favourite teachers, but shake their heads each time. Korka suggests Aron's special helper at school, to which Aron shakes his head even more vigorously. Korka names her defence-class instructor, Mrs. Alpern, then says, "Nah."

"We don't need anyone," Jon says in a defeated tone.

Aron gives him a thumbs-up.

"Then we go it alone," Korka says.

"Can't."

"Can," she says. "I know where Mom's and Dad's wallets are, and I know their bank-card PINs."

"What? You sneak. How ... like, you spied on them when they were at the banking machine?"

"Uh-huh."

"Have you actually taken their cards and used them before?"

She lowers her head. "Once, and I only took out a little."

"Did they notice?"

"They're both useless with money," Korka says, shaking her head.

"And how would you know that?" Jon says, amazed.

"I just do." She shrugs.

Aron frowns and punches her arm lightly. Her face crumples.

"Korka," Jon says, watching tears slide down her pale cheeks. "I'm going down to their office to sort through stuff. I'll distract Mrs. Vine while you go out the back door, dodge the reporters, and get to a bank machine. Take out whatever the card lets you. We'll max it once every day until the money runs out or someone freezes their accounts. Because we're going to need money soon, even if Mrs. Vine brings over some food."

She stops sniffling and looks at him. "We should face the reporters and tell them to go away, so we don't *have* to sneak out."

Impressed at her courage, Jon nods. "Okay, we'll face them together and tell them where to go. Aron, you coming?"

Aron pulls the pillows in front of his face.

Jon and Korka make a quick plan. They pad downstairs and nod on the way past Mrs. Vine. Then Korka fakes tripping on a rug and landing on her stomach.

"Oh, darling, are you okay?" their caretaker asks, shutting off the vacuum cleaner and rushing to lean over Korka. The second Mrs. Vine's back is turned to him, Jon moves to the coat rack by the front door, retrieves both

Mom's and Dad's wallets, and slips them into Korka's parka pocket.

"Stupid rug. But I'm fine," Korka says, hopping up and brushing herself off.

"Sure?" Jon asks in a concerned way.

"No worries," Korka responds. "We're going to speak to the reporters," Jon tells Mrs. Vine.

"Are you sure that's a good idea?" she asks, frowning.

"Yes." They don their coats, hold hands, open the front door, and step out onto the porch.

Jon gulps at the sight of half a dozen bundled-up reporters from out of town, standing in front of this log house occupied by a family no one cared about till this morning. Cameras are lifted, microphones are stuck in their faces, and people start barking questions.

"How are you coping?"

"Is it true you performed CPR on your own mother?"

"Why would both your mother and father, who run a survival school, enter a high-risk avalanche zone without avalanche beacons?"

"Will there be an inquiry?"

"Who will look after you? Where will you go?"

Jon is struck dumb. What was he thinking to step outside? He wants all these reporters to burn in hell for their hurtful questions.

"We are survivors. We'll get through this together," Korka says, eyes flashing, voice rising.

Trust Korka to give them what for! But as they turn to her, she lowers her head and begins crying. Jon senses the cameras zooming in. His tongue finally loosens.

"We ask you to give us privacy at this time." With that, he and Korka reach for the door handle together, back up into the house, and double-bolt the door again.

"Good job," Jon says, hugging her.

"Well done, kids," Mrs. Vine says, eyebrows arched as she stands awkwardly in the kitchen doorway.

Korka buries her head in Jon's chest for a moment, then heads for the back door. She darts out so fast that he feels sorry for anyone who tries to accost her on her mission.

"Where's she going?" Mrs. Vine asks, alarm in her tone.

"Just out to pick up some snacks. She'll be back in a minute," Jon says, resenting their neighbour's presence already.

He checks on Aron, tells him Korka will be back in a few minutes, and parks himself in Mom and Dad's office with Amanda's brochure in hand. He also phones Mark, who offers to come over.

"Thanks, but not now," Jon tells him, chest so tight an elk could be sitting on it. They talk for a while. Mark sounds like he actually understands what it feels like to have all the light go out of the world.

Hours later, deep into the night, Korka and Jon sit in the office, sorting files. Mrs. Vine snores on the futon, manicured toenails dangling out from under a long yellow flannel nightgown. Korka opens a small drawer in Dad's desk, runs her hand along the underside of the drawer above it, and removes a key taped there.

"For the safe," she whispers.

"You're way too qualified for a life of crime," Jon whispers back.

In the safe are insurance forms, birth certificates, passports, and a small stack of cash. They add the money to what Korka brought home and place it in an empty coffee can.

The next morning, by the time they eat their brunch — Mrs. Vine overboils the eggs — Jon figures they've satisfied most of the items on the brochure's checklist, a few with Mrs. Vine's help. Finally, their would-be guardian steps out to check on her own household.

That's when Jon directs Aron to get busy pulling all the food out of the cupboards in the house and garage and listing them on a pad of paper.

Minutes later, as Jon continues the Google research he began the night before, he cries out. "Says here the average funeral costs ten thousand dollars. And that's for just *one* person!"

"Then search *low-cost funeral*," Korka advises in a choked voice.

Mrs. Vine returns, checks on them, and heads out to buy groceries. That gives them enough time to get the funeral cost down to twenty-five hundred dollars by following the advice they find on the internet. First, Jon calls the hospital to have the bodies released directly to a crematorium. Evidently that eliminates coffin, embalming, and viewing costs. Second, they use social media and a call to the local paper to announce a memorial in the local park, rather than offering a catered event.

As the day advances to night, and despite Mrs. Vine's presence, Korka has crying jags now and again. Each time, Aron runs back upstairs to hide. Mrs. Vine never follows the boy, and anybody's attempts to calm Korka result in her pulling or running away. Her tears make Jon want to cry himself, but he is determined to hold it together for his siblings' sakes. More than anything, he feels limp, heavy, and filled with a nameless pain. He wants to run out onto the mountain and breathe life into his parents' bodies, even though their bodies aren't there anymore. Once again, he blocks out those unbelievable, horrible moments he spent in the chilly morgue identifying their bodies, Officer Vine silent at his side.

At least the reporters have left.

Neighbours have dropped off food. Many emails have arrived that Jon can't bear to read. Instead, he emails cancellations to the four people signed up for the next survival course. He ignores the messages from the Rockvale couple wanting to track down their runaway teen, Leah Green. He does search for her name on the school's registration lists and learns she took an advanced wilderness-survival course from his parents last summer.

"Look at this pile of bills," he moans, shaking his head. "Heat, electricity, rent, and phone bills all overdue."

Memories come to him of his father bent over the computer each evening, hands in his hair, face grey, papers strewn all over his desk. And his mother softly calling him to bed. Did he leave the house with a faulty beacon because he was so distracted and stressed by their ongoing financial situation?

"But according to the internet," Korka says, "survivors don't have to pay off the debt. Credit card companies write it off after taking what's in the bank and what the assets sell for. Wait. Depends on … oh, this is so confusing."

"There's just the truck," Jon says, fingering an unpaid bill for its latest repairs. "And there's no will," he says tiredly. "Been through absolutely everything now."

The doorbell rings. Korka sprints to the door. "Go home!" she hollers through the cedar panels.

"It's Amanda," comes the patient reply.

SIX

When Jon and Korka hesitate, Aron leaps up to let in their social worker. He's a little surprised when she sheds her boots, seats herself in an overstuffed armchair, and pulls a form out of her purple briefcase before even saying hello. He watches her closely, trying to decide if she's trustworthy or not. He has a knack for reading people. It's a young-Viking superpower granted as a birthright by Nordic deities, which he simply accepts.

"Mrs. Vine is out grocery shopping," Jon informs their visitor. "We searched Mom and Dad's office, went on the internet, and took care of everything on your brochure list — except there's no will."

Aron isn't sure what a will is or does, but he pictures a medieval scroll hidden in a secret drawer of a castle keep.

As Korka and Jon fill Amanda in on all the details, she focuses kind blue eyes on Aron, who pretends not to know this. Instead, he busies himself lining up food like he's building a Nordic fort. A very small fort, given the limited supply of food. The kingdom is on the brink of starvation, which could lead to revolt.

"Good job, Aron," Amanda says, startling him.

"Thank you," Aron replies evenly. He already knows he's doing an excellent job, of course. Jon and Korka raise their eyebrows, like they didn't expect him to speak in front of a stranger. They also know it's his code for ruling her okay.

"But keep the canned stuff in a pile separate from the other things," Jon suggests.

Aron frowns. That's Jon trying to show the social worker that he rules over his clan.

"Let Aron do it his way," Korka says, a little too loudly.

And that's Korka objecting to Jon's acting superior, as opposed to actually sticking up for a younger brother.

Amanda winks at Aron — an interesting omen implying she may read minds — and says, "Well done with the paperwork, Jon and Korka. You're making things remarkably easy for your guardian."

"We don't have a guardian," Jon says. The room goes quiet and tense.

Aron joins Jon and Korka on the couch. Maintaining a face as neutral as a citadel guard, he waits eagerly to see Amanda's response to that.

Her lips press together. She places the form on the coffee table between them and offers Jon a pen, smiling encouragingly. She's wearing loose jeans, a T-shirt that reads *Support Your Local Search & Rescue Team*, and wool toe socks with each toe in a different colour. Aron likes her socks, even if he would not wish them for himself.

"What happens if we don't sign this?" Jon asks, resting his arms along the sofa back, above Korka's and Aron's shoulders. *How about asking your immediate clansmen for opinions, Big Viking?* Aron thinks. But he's not inclined to say it aloud, these being matters of gravity and high dominion.

"We're still working to verify that you have no relatives, but assuming that's correct, then you would deal with the government instead of with the Vines. And you are even more likely to be split up as we search for foster homes. There's also the option of going to a group home, which you definitely want to avoid." Her eyes meet each of theirs with a steadiness Aron has to turn away from. "I have not heard from you with an alternative guardian, and no one else has come forward."

Despite the playful toe socks, she's pretty stern, Aron decides.

"Can you give us another few days?" Aron dares to ask before Big Viking speaks.

"Or weeks?" Korka says cheekily.

Amanda sighs. "I can give you until the end of the week, provided Mrs. Vine continues to stay with you. She says she's willing to."

"Perfect," Jon says, rising slowly. "See you at the end of the week, then."

In other words, if there has to be a spy, Mrs. Vine's okay.

"You know where to reach me," this Amanda lady says, her voice a little chillier now. She snaps her briefcase shut, leaving the piece of paper lying on the coffee table beside their mother's half-finished jigsaw puzzle of a rainbow. "I'm sorry," she says in a kinder tone, "but it is my job to ensure we are all adhering to the law."

"Thank you," Jon says.

Aron nods politely, but he's so weary that he can barely find the energy to see her to the door. He let her in. His job to let her out. Then pull up the drawbridge.

She slips her colourful feet into the furry boots that match Mom's, which have been returned and are sitting beside the closet door as if waiting for their owner. If Aron pushes them into the closet, he somehow fears she'll never come home.

When the front door shuts, Aron turns and looks at Jon. "We could run away," Aron states, mouth gone dry. The notion of a clandestine adventure intrigues and beckons. It doesn't scare a warrior like himself.

Jon nods slowly, like he has thought of this already. "We could hide in the woods where no one can find us. No one would be better at that than us. Mom and Dad have a huge supply of dehydrated and freeze-dried food in a locker in the garage. We could backpack into an old mining community Dad and I hiked into once, a ghost town with empty houses. It's several weeks' hike from a trailhead just north of here. We could live there and fish and snare for food."

"We'd be dropping out of school before the end of the year," Korka says, her brow wrinkled. "Which means you won't graduate, Jon."

"Clan ties are more important," Aron rules.

"True, Young Viking. And it'll be easy for us to make up the assignments we miss when we come back," Jon says calmly. "But cops and Search and Rescue might try to come after us. We'll be on the run."

Aron notes that Jon and Korka turn to him. He studies the kitchen table for several long minutes. "We can dodge them," he finally rules. "The Vikings will triumph."

"You sure, Aron?" Jon's face is grave. "We're talking weeks of walking through difficult brush with huge packs on our backs, no roads or cities nearby, camping, snaring, fishing, going hungry sometimes, maybe meeting dangerous animals, putting up with nasty weather, and hiding from whoever. All three of us have to agree to that, and all three of us have to get along."

"Yes," Aron says, more confidently this time. He holds both thumbs up and gives his siblings a twitch of a smile. "Armed with swords and daggers, we will work our way through the labyrinth."

Jon smiles at Korka. "That's quite the mouthful from our Nordic-legend fanatic. But he's on target." He pauses and goes solemn. "Survival. We can do it better than any kids I know. Okay, pop quiz. What are the highest-calorie, lightest-weight backpacking foods, in order, please?"

"Oil, nuts and seeds, coconut milk powder, powdered eggs, freeze-dried beans, Parmesan cheese, and meat jerky," Korka recites, tossing her braid over her shoulder.

"Chocolate," Aron adds.

"Correct. We can carry only so much weight, so —"

"— everything we take has to give us at least five calories per gram," Aron finishes proudly.

"Exactly," Jon says. "Dehydrated food weighs less than freeze-dried, but we'll need some of both. We need twenty-five hundred calories per day, so that means we each need about five hundred grams of food every day. I can carry about twenty-five kilograms, and you two, maybe ten kilos each. If food is sixty percent of our packs, what we can carry will last us less than five weeks, so we'll have to find other stuff to eat along the way. And we'll have to build campfires a lot so we don't have to carry more fuel. But we'll survive. We will make it till my birthday!"

His rambling math makes Aron smile a little shakily.

"Here's the locker key," Jon says, turning to Aron. "Help Korka with sorting."

Two days later, Jon shivers under a grey sky in the park. The memorial service seems to have brought out the whole town and then some. He and his siblings form a short lineup of three hunched figures. Aron's the bravest of all for even being there, never mind that he's also the one gripping the pottery jar Jon and Korka chose to hold their parents' remains. Slumped between them, Aron clings to the jar, never lifting his eyes from the melting snow around their boots.

Mark appears in front of them, brown curls peeking out from under his backward baseball cap, goofy smile toned down for the day. Jon accepts his hug awkwardly but appreciatively.

When Korka's Krav Maga teacher, Mrs. Alpern, engulfs her in a tight bear hug, Jon watches his sister lose it. Her favourite adult, for sure.

"What can I do?" Mrs. Alpern whispers. Her eyes are puffy.

"Nothing, but thanks," Jon says.

"If you change your mind, you know where I am," she says. She hugs each of them, then walks away, head hung low.

Jon and Korka spend the rest of the hour shaking hands with an endless parade of people, many they don't know. *Sorry for your loss, sorry for your loss, sorry for your loss.* Jon bites his lip, worrying he'll explode if he hears the words one more time.

He jumps a little as Officer Vine appears, leans forward, and grips his hand. "We'll talk Friday, Jon. We'll keep helping you through everything you and your family are facing."

"Thanks," Jon says. *For nothing.*

Mrs. Vine, weeping, hugs Korka, while Jon's date from hell brushes her lips on his cheek, her eyelashes wet, eyes downcast. Neither Jon nor Korka respond. Jon's body, feet, and soul feel entirely numb. He figures Korka's feeling the same. Aron is leaning hard against Korka's frame, looking ready to collapse.

Jon stares up at the cool grey sky and wishes with all his being for his parents to stop this charade and come home. His heart is broken into ten thousand pieces.

SEVEN

After Mrs. Vine drops them off in their driveway and promises to be over in an hour, they open the door to discover there's no heat or light in the house. Jon rushes to the computer. Limited battery power left. He checks the phones. Same.

"Damn" is all he can say, as Korka and Aron run around lighting the candles, kerosene lanterns, and battery lamps they use for power outages. And yet, given what he learned as he and Korka riffled through paperwork earlier, Jon guesses this isn't a power outage. It's because of the unpaid bills.

Aron starts building a fire in the fireplace like the expert he is. Jon flashes back to an overnight backpacking trip many autumns ago. Aron at age four was still small enough to be in a child carrier on their mom's strong back, though he'd walk for a while between periods of being carried. Jon remembers Korka skipping beside their mother and making faces at her little brother, prompting Aron to giggle as they walked along in the fresh mountain air.

A wicked thunderstorm let loose at some point, the heavy rain soaking every pine needle and patch of earth in their entire world. Their dad ushered them under the shelter of a rock overhang, where they put on their rain ponchos and waited for it to let up.

"A rainbow!" Korka called out to Aron a while later, expecting him to be thrilled by the hazy arc of colour on the horizon. "Vikings called rainbows *bifröst*, which means 'shimmering path.' Right, Mom? Tell us the story."

"Rainbows are burning bridges that reach from Earth to the realm of the gods," Mom began, patting Korka's damp hair.

"And there's a pot of gold —" Korka enthused.

"Actually, that's an Irish thing."

Meanwhile, Aron seemed entirely focused on crawling about the little cave, picking up dead aspen leaves that had blown in. He collected a small pile, which he guarded like it was a pot of gold.

"Yucky," Jon told him, yanking a brittle leaf from his small, chubby hand.

That made the boy's face pinch up like he was going to cry. But instead, he picked up another leaf, crumbled it in one hand, and caught its pieces in his other palm like he was sifting. Then he stuffed the mess into his rain poncho pocket.

"Let him play," Mom said. "They're just leaves."

That night, after they had set up camp under a still-dripping sky, Dad asked, "Who's going to light the fire tonight?"

Jon stepped forward proudly and tried, but the kindling he had gathered was too damp to spark. He was frustrated enough to kick over his pyramid of sticks.

"Korka?" their mom asked patiently. Korka tried and tried, and finally burst into tears. "Impossible!" she protested. "It's too wet! You do it! We want marshmallows!"

As usual, Dad launched into a lecture about gathering tinder in dry conditions and keeping some in a plastic bag for wet days. He went on and on about the kinds of wood to avoid because they smoulder rather than burn: alder, chestnut, poplar, and willow. Then he reminded them that mixing wood chips and grass with animal poop makes for long-burning fires, which made Korka wrinkle her nose and giggle.

"Okay," their father finally said. "I'll start the fire, and you all watch."

But Aron, free of the child carrier, walked over and tapped his father's elbow. "Me," he insisted.

Mom and Dad, winking at each other, said, "Sure, Aron. Go for it."

To everyone's amazement, Aron built a fire teepee from scratch, sprinkling his precious leaf bits on it with a look of intense concentration, then accepting the match Mom reluctantly handed him. He lit the fire on his first attempt. He fanned the initial glow, then sat back and grinned as everyone clapped and patted him on the back.

"You have a gift," Mom said softly.

"You're amazing," Dad said.

And ever since, Aron had been the first to volunteer for fire starting, and the one who always succeeded the fastest.

Now, as the candles flicker and the kindling in the fireplace crackles, Jon places his arms around Aron's shoulders. In the leaping flames, he sees their parents smiling proudly, like they did at the camp that night. The flames fail to warm a sadness that suffuses his entire being. But he must shake himself out of that.

"We have twenty-four hours before Amanda's back," Jon reminds them, stretching his arms toward the hearth's steady blaze. "We have enough wood for the fireplace till then. And for supper, we've got casseroles the neighbours brought."

Aron heads for the kitchen.

They eat the rubbery lasagna Mrs. Vine made for them the night before and divide up some thawed spinach. Mrs. Vine arrives, her eyes, as usual, darting about to avoid looking at them too much, or maybe to identify household chores that immediately need doing. She keeps her coat on as she tsk-tsks about the "power outage."

"I think you need to sleep at my house tonight," she says cautiously, as if fearful of their reaction.

"We just need this one last night here together," Korka begs sweetly.

Aron follows this up by standing in front of Mrs. Vine, palms pressed together like he's praying. She takes a step backward, as if he's got a disease she might catch.

Then she looks about before saying, "Well, Jon, you've got the fire going, anyway. What would these two do without you? Oh dear, you might run out of firewood. I'll just run home again and bring some back." And she hurries out the door.

Jon's not about to remind her they have a plentiful supply in the garage. He lets her leave.

"Should've told her you're the real fire starter," Korka says, putting her arm around Aron. Aron beams.

"Yeah." Jon slides an arm around Aron from the other side.

Jon phones up Mark to firm up their plans.

"You don't have to do this," Mark says. "You can hang out at my house, or —"

"It's all decided, Mark," Jon says firmly.

"Yeah, I get that," Mark says more warmly. "Well, it'll be one hell of an adventure. Almost wish I could come along. But you can always phone me if you get in trouble."

"I know. Thanks, Mark." Jon will miss his best friend, no question. But this crisis isn't about Mark. He and Korka and Aron have to do this themselves.

Jon watches his sister and brother arrange the giant packs of food, water, and gear in the garage, like they have for extended backcountry trips a hundred times before.

The only difference is there's no Mom and Dad to enthuse over their hard work, or to double-check it. Korka slips out to the grocery store to spend some of their coffee-can money on last-minute essentials. The bank machine doesn't work anymore.

Jon uses the dying laptop to check their planned route to the abandoned mining town, where they can hopefully hole up unseen until his birthday. From there, it's a two-day hike over a mountain pass into the tiny nearby town of Wolfsburg — elevation 1,100 metres — for supplies.

As he deletes everything on the computer, Jon looks around the house and feels the first stirrings of anger. *Why did you do this to us, Mom and Dad? We need you. I need you. You expect me to look after everyone on my own? At my age?*

He stares at the personalized calendar on the wall over the desk, then begins to turn its pages one by one. There's a happy family photo of the five of them for each month, one on a mountain peak, one with them tobogganing. In another, they're a pyramid of laughing bodies in front of a tent in springtime. He pauses on the month of June. It features a photo of all five grinning at the camera from the dock of a scenic mountain lake, each holding up a fishing rod.

He flips back to May. The eighth, his eighteenth birthday, is circled, suggesting a grand family celebration had been planned. Maybe an extra-special trip into the mountains, where they'd have feasted on Mom's picnic-basket goodies, played Frisbee as mountain goats picked their way along a cliff high above, relaxed in a meadow of wild-flowers with eagles soaring overhead. He rips the calendar off the wall, tears it into what seems like a thousand pieces, then tosses the bits into a wastebasket. He sucks in air to halt tears.

By the time Mrs. Vine returns, they've parked their fully loaded truck two blocks from the house and locked the garage securely.

"Good night, Mrs. Vine," they each say as they traipse up to bed.

At midnight, his alarm and the sound of Mark's rusty Chevrolet passing the house wake Jon at the same time. Sweating, he rouses Korka and Aron, who went to bed fully clothed. The three of them slide down a tied sheet out of their parents' bedroom window and all but tiptoe the two blocks to their truck.

Mark pulls up behind them. They silently trans-fer three gargantuan packs into Mark's trunk, then pile themselves into the Gunnarsson truck. With a big sigh and a lingering look toward their log home, Jon starts driving. He heads for the highway and turns south, with Mark following.

"They'll fall for it," Korka reassures him. Aron leans into her sleepily.

It was Mark's idea to abandon their beat-up Nissan at the nearest city bus station in the middle of the night. Isn't that where most kids would head if running away?

But they're all a little choked up as they leave the old pickup there and climb into Mark's ride.

They now head in the opposite direction, north, on the wet black asphalt flanked by snowbanks. The dotted centreline blurs as Mark and Jon talk in low tones over Korka's and Aron's snoring.

Aron, Jon notices, is gripping the slingshot Dad helped him make from a deer antler and surgical tubing. Korka is wearing Mom's Swiss Army knife on a chain around her neck. For a moment, he feels bummed that he has taken none of his parents' belongings to remember them by.

Then he remembers he has his father's homemade bone-handle hunting knife — and most important of all, his siblings.

EIGHT

When Mark drops them off at the remote northern trail-head, they stand outside his car for a few minutes. Aron yawns and leans against Korka. Jon is both reluctant to say goodbye and anxious to get going.

"Sure I can't talk you out of this?" Mark asks one more time.

"No, Mark, but thanks." Jon tries to push gas money into his friend's hands.

"No way, bro. Not taking it," Mark insists. "Bad enough to be an accomplice. Could get arrested or something for this." He laughs a little nervously. "Anyway, I won't say a word to anyone. Get in touch anytime if there's ever an emergency or anything."

"Sure," Jon says, though they both know the Gunnarssons have brought neither phone nor computer with them, and wouldn't get reception out here even if they had. Jon tucks the money back into the tight-lidded coffee can that holds their stash and zips it into his backpack. "We'll be back May eighth."

"Your birthday." Mark nods.

Two and a half months. *A lifetime*, Jon thinks. An owl hoots in the dark, frosty forest.

"Korka, Aron, look after your brother," Mark says, clapping Jon on the back. He climbs into his Chevy.

Jon raises a hand numbly as the vehicle backs away and takes off down the road, red taillights shrinking like his confidence. He tries to picture his parents pulling up in a few minutes to join them. All that does is tighten his chest and threaten to unleash tears.

Jon watches Aron's big tears fall silently down his cheeks, despite his brother trying to wipe them away.

"It's three of us now," Jon tries to reassure his siblings, "and what counts is that we're all strong and brave and together. Proud of you, Aron," he adds as his brother struggles into an adult-sized backpack and turns on his headlamp.

As he leads his two siblings down the dark, snow-covered trail, Jon's bursting-at-the-seams pack feels like it has the weight of the world in it. And yet, he feels an excitement not quite smothered by the cloud of grief and fear. Like his dad, he has always loved testing himself outdoors:

heading out on his own, with only basic necessities, even in storms. Especially in storms. Endurance trials can be an addictive game. He and Mark, who shares that passion, have had some epic adventures as a result, valuable learning experiences, even if they freaked out their parents.

Then he feels a flash of guilt for even thinking of survival as a game right now, and he grits his teeth. With Korka and Aron along, no one but Mark having a clue where they are, and no safety net of a home or parents to return to, this is no game.

Jon glances behind to see Korka reach for Aron's hand, but their little brother shakes free, cocking his head as he listens to the quiet blackness around them. Aron ploughs ahead of them both in the chilly windless night, like he's the designated leader. Jon smiles and keeps a stride behind. "Never underestimate Aron," their mom always said.

The kid is probably imagining himself as one of the mythical Norse heroes in his books and games, Jon figures. And why not? It would be a good way to escape the crushing reality of their new situation and to bolster his courage.

A short while later, they pitch their little green tent on a snowy plateau off the trail, string up their food pack between two giant lodgepole pines to keep predators from reaching it, and crawl toward their waterproof, breathable down sleeping bags. Jon guesses he's not the only one pretending that their parents' tent is right beside theirs.

Jon zips up the door and wriggles into his sleeping bag. "Not enough room in here," grumps Korka.

Before he can think of a smart response, Jon's asleep.

The sun has been up for hours by the time Jon prods them awake. "Gotta move, guys. We need to get as far away from the road as we can before dark today. Once we're discovered missing, there might be searchers scouring the area to find us."

"Not moving," the hump in Korka's sleeping bag mumbles. "Too cold. Too tired."

"Last one up doesn't get breakfast," Jon says, stirring the pot of instant oatmeal he has made on their tiny backpacking stove just outside the tent flaps.

He tries to hold off the questions building up inside him. How many weeks will the stove fuel last? And their food supplies? Not all the way till his birthday, that's for sure. But it's too early to worry about hunting, fishing, and a resupply trip to Wolfsburg.

At least for now they're safe, together, and well equipped (thanks to Mom and Dad's supplies) with everything from water-purification tablets, a folding saw, and a compass, to a top-of-the-line medical kit. Before they left, he searched thoroughly and frantically for the family's GPS, but never did find it. Also, each of them wears a whistle around their neck for emergencies. And Jon has accepted the mantle of leadership. He will provide for and protect his family, whatever it takes.

"Cinnamon," Aron declares, sniffing at the bowl of oatmeal Jon hands him.

Korka sits up, and they all exchange pained looks. They don't need to be reminded of the name of Dad's last ski run, not this morning.

"And almonds and apple slices," Jon says quickly, kneeling at the tent entrance with two more steaming bowls. Korka shrugs off her sleeping bag enough to warm her palms with the bowl he serves her. Jon settles down with his own bowl.

"So, after breakfast each day," Jon says, "Korka washes dishes in the stream, Aron takes down and packs up the tent, and I'll clean the site. It's important we all pull our weight — and that we don't leave any traces behind."

"Who made you commander-in-chief?" Korka snaps.

Jon pauses, startled, then continues rattling off the list he has carefully constructed. "In the evenings, I dig the toilet hole with the portable trowel if the ground isn't too frozen. Otherwise it's a designated ring of rocks. I haul big firewood pieces, Korka gathers kindling, I chop wood, and Aron starts the fire. Korka fetches water or melts snow, I cook the food, Korka washes dishes, and I hang the food bag up so the bears and such don't claw into it. Hanging the food bag correctly is the most important job. Oh, except for erasing all signs of our campsite when we move on. We'll need to fool any skilled trackers with all the tricks we know, every step of the way."

He watches Aron leap up proudly and start to eject sleeping bags and pads from the tent.

"Hey, careful you don't get stuff damp or dirty," Jon says. "And don't push the tent poles into their bag too roughly or they'll make a hole."

Aron frowns but carries on.

Korka tosses pine cones at a nearby tree trunk. "You think fetching water and washing dishes are a girl's job, don't you?" she says in a snarky tone. "And I know why you're claiming any chore to do with food. It's 'cause you don't trust us not to sneak extra when we get hungry. But I'm as good as you at chopping wood, and you suck at cooking."

Jon grimaces. Does she have to do this now? Well, he's not about to back down. They need order and routine on this trip.

"Fetching water is important," he says in what he hopes is a stern voice. "Everyone packs up their own personal stuff. Now, let's see how much distance we can knock off today. If we hear anyone or if helicopters fly overhead, dive into the nearest underbrush. We need to be on alert for pursuers all the way to the mining town."

"Are the houses haunted in the ghost town?" Aron asks as he slides the last of the tent pegs into their bag.

"Of course not," Korka says. "Remember Dad showed us a book with photos of the place when miners actually lived there? Women in long skirts and big hats and funny little black boots with buttons, pushing white baby buggies. I remember small wooden houses, each with its own garden and white picket fence. We can choose the best house and plant our own garden. Right, Jon? And get water from a well, just like they did back then. We'll have the whole town to ourselves!"

Jon smiles. "Sounds good, but remember no one has lived there for forty years, so there's lots of broken windows and rotted flooring. And Dad says — said — backpackers sometimes camp there on their way farther into the mountains. We'll have to hide if anyone shows. But we'll make do, and you two can help choose our house."

"It'll be one with curtains still in it," Korka muses. "Lace curtains flapping in the breeze, and an old wood stove ready to light."

Jon raises an eyebrow but doesn't comment, given that he's basically lost when it comes to understanding fourteen-year-old girls. Or girls in general, it seems.

Soon the three of them are packed up and moving along the frozen path, alert expeditioners each carrying way more than their usual load.

"Nice we don't need snowshoes," Korka observes.

The rhythmic *crunch, crunch* of their boots on the snow keeps Jon's mind off the hole in his heart.

"It's almost spring," she adds. "So, no snow pretty soon, right?"

"First of all, we're not so close to spring that we can rule out a late snowstorm," Jon says. "The valley we're headed for is at over thirteen hundred metres elevation — one thousand, three hundred and seventy-two metres, to be precise — and the hike will take us on lots of ups and downs. We'll get everything from snow and ice to mud and mosquitoes." He's proud he studied the topographical map beforehand, including the contours their dad taught them to interpret for elevation and steepness. "But so will anyone chasing us," he adds solemnly.

A brilliant bowl of blue hovers above them, and the pine-needle-strewn trail winds through endless stands of lodgepole pine and white spruce. Jon tries to set a pace that pushes them without making Aron huff. Not that Aron's the complaining type. Jon watches the sweat on his little brother's brow, his chin thrust forward. As usual, the kid is keyed into the forest sounds as if they're directed only at him.

Canada jays dance in the branches above, and a downy woodpecker *rat-a-tats* from a trunk high overhead. Mom and Dad would be pointing out all that stuff if they were along. But Jon doesn't have the energy to do it today. His memories of family hikes give him an ache like a bear has swatted his side.

"Think we'll run into any other hikers?" Korka asks Jon, adjusting the straps on her heavy pack.

"Hopefully not this time of year. If we do hear any-one, remember, we hide in the trees or brush," Jon says. "Otherwise, talk or sing quietly as we come around blind corners, and stay close together, so we don't sur-prise a cougar or moose or bear, though bears are still hibernating for now. That would be worse than acciden-tally meeting a hiker."

He touches the can of pepper spray on his belt, and beside it the leather sheath holding Dad's bone-handle knife. Aron raises the slingshot he carries around his neck, as if to announce he will protect them.

"And I'll scare 'em off with my moves," Korka jokes.

As they walk, she whips up some Norse tales from Aron's favourite books to keep him moving. He turns his face up to her. *A wounded fawn in need of a mother*, Jon thinks, *despite the brave front he's keeping up*.

They pause for lunch at a breathtaking viewpoint. They spend a few minutes gazing over a snowy valley covered in straight-backed lodgepole pines. Then Jon pulls out the map and pores over their route as Korka makes peanut-butter-and-jelly sandwiches and hands them out.

"You could thank me, you know." Her voice cuts into his concentration.

"Huh? Yeah, thanks, Korka," he replies.

When he rises, just moments after they've finished eating, Korka and Aron take it as the signal to pack stuff away and fall back into position. Jon walks over to re-adjust Korka's straps.

"They're already fine, bossy boss." Korka's sarcastic tone again.

Who's not thanking who now? he thinks, but doesn't bother taking the bait.

NINE

As the threesome marches ahead, Korka holds Aron's hand tightly. That suits Jon fine. She's Aron's "little mother," as Mom is always saying. *Was* saying. And now, Jon reflects with a lump in his throat, she's his *only* mother.

"Three," Jon says from up ahead, like they're playing I Spy or something. Their family used to do this on long hikes to keep the kids moving or stop them from fighting. "Third time lucky. Three-leaf clover."

"Three," Aron announces from behind them. "A lucky number. Norse symbol of valknut."

Korka scratches her head. "If you catch a leprechaun and set him free, he grants you three wishes."

"That's Irish. We're Icelandic," Aron says, wrinkling his nose.

"Not everything we do has to be about Vikings," Korka retorts. "You're so weird, Aron."

"Important things come in threes," Aron persists.

"Whatever you say, Young Viking," Korka says, rolling her eyes.

"The Norse myth of the three Norns," her little brother says patiently, "is about phases of the moon."

"It's daytime, silly. No moon up there," Korka says, "waxing, waning, or whatever.

"You're all waning. Try to step it up," says Jon.

Korka run-walks until she passes Jon, forcing him to keep his eye on Aron for a turn. She keeps up the brisk pace as if needing to prove she's strong and fit. Or maybe, like him, she's pretending they're on a weekend hike that has nothing to do with losing Mom and Dad, or with hiding from searchers.

Hours later, their quiet world is shattered by the sudden sound of helicopter blades approaching. Even before Jon shouts a warning, his siblings dive into a thicket like it's a well-practised manoeuvre.

"We're just being careful," Korka says casually to Aron. She draws his shaking frame to hers. "Probably no one looking for us yet. Especially not here."

"Yet," Jon repeats under his breath. He starts when Aron begins thrashing beside him, and crying out. "What's wrong, Aron?" He tries to cup his brother's body against his own, but Aron only fights harder.

"His claustrophobia," Korka says.

Of course. Jon loosens his grip on his brother and pulls him to where a beam of sunlight shines into the dense bushes, which seems to calm him. But it brings unwelcome memories and a stab of guilt for Jon, who knows all too well how Aron came to fear small, dark spaces — and why he seldom speaks.

It started five years ago, on a blue-sky winter day in their little mountain town. He and his siblings got bored with making a snowman in their backyard. So, when their mother wasn't looking out the kitchen window, they wandered up the slippery slope.

Jon, twelve at the time, was bursting with a need to prove he was a great and brave explorer. "What, you can't keep up?" he prodded them. "Are you scaredy-cats? Wait till you see the jewels in the magic cave!"

"No way!" huffed nine-year-old Korka, increasing her pace as sweat ran down her brow below her pink-and-white parka hood.

Aron, age six, widened his eyes and smiled. "I want to see the jewels!"

Tall and gangly for his age, Jon led them past a scrawled cardboard sign that pronounced *Stay out!* Then they clambered over orange net fencing and crawled under yellow tape.

Huh! Jon thought. *The older boys think they can keep me out with that?* And he lifted his eyes toward the very cool snow cave the boys had been building in a giant snowbank on the edge of town.

At last, the three stood, bundled in their coats, boots, and handknit wool hats, inside the head-high white chamber. Jon's heart was doing double time. The cave was big enough for two tall adults to lie end to end from the entrance to the rear. He reached out to touch the rippled walls, which were diamond-bright with moisture.

Korka clomped over to four cozy nooks carved into the snow walls. "Beds!" she enthused, lying down on one of the benches and folding her hands behind her hood.

Aron pointed to a dark space at the rear leading to who knew where. "A tunnel." He spoke in almost a whisper. The smooth, flat floor sloped like a skating rink toward the tunnel.

Jon lifted his head in awe to take in the light shimmering through the thin snow of the high arched roof. Water droplets sparkled like sequins. "So cool," Jon said. It was way cooler than he'd expected. But this magical place also reeked of danger. What if the older boys caught them trespassing? He shivered.

"Where are the jewels?" Aron asked.

"He just made that up to get you here." Korka sniffed.

"They're in the next cave." Jon released Aron's hand to tickle him.

"This is like a marble palace!" Korka said. She pointed to the arched ceiling, below which Jon spied a carved-out shelf. It held a deck of cards, and someone had poked a stick into the shelf to hang a lantern.

"The walls look like whipped cream," Korka said, poking her finger into the surface and tasting the moisture. She pointed at water dripping from the ceiling. "But it's melting."

"The jewels are down there?" Aron asked, pointing a wavering finger toward the dark-throated tunnel.

"Maybe," said Jon.

"The floor is kind of tilted, like a slide." Korka leapt off her snow bench and peered toward the shadowy rear.

"Let's scratch our initials on the wall." Jon reached for the Swiss Army knife in his parka pocket.

"Whee!" Aron shouted, dropping to his bottom and sliding away from his siblings.

"No!" Jon and Korka shrieked.

But a heartbeat after their little brother disappeared into the dark tunnel, they heard a loud thud, followed by a groan from the snowy walls. A clump of wet snow fell from the roof, landing with a splat in front of the tunnel entrance.

Jon grabbed Korka to pull her out of the cave, but instantly sensed they wouldn't make it to the entrance in time. So, as the ghostly walls began to shift and spill out chunks, he pushed her to the ground beneath him and covered both their heads with his arms. His body trembled as the ceiling released clods of snow the size of roof tiles. Then it rained larger, concrete-hard blocks onto his back.

With an eerie rumbling, the cave continued to collapse, pressing them into the body-chilling floor. The cold seemed to burn as it covered their bodies and filled their nostrils. Fear gripped him from head to toe, but, having heard many avalanche safety lectures from his parents over the years, Jon knew to kick and flail his arms like a swimmer to create space for breathing and breaking out.

When things fell quiet again, he tried to move against the heavy giant that pinned him and his sister to the floor. Not easy. Refusing to panic, he punched upward and wriggled until enough of the cold wetness fell away from his mouth that he could breathe. His face now stuck out of a mound of snow in a roofless cavern.

"Korka?" he called as he crawled forward off of her. He kept calling her name as he pulled her from the cement-like mix.

"Uhh," she responded, tears melting the slush on her face.

"Get out while I grab Aron!" he ordered, sliding down a portion of the snow tongue to the tunnel entrance, now a wall of solid white. "Aron?" he shouted.

No answer.

He turned into a boxer, pummelling the wall, digging, yanking snow away, freezing his fists, attempting to tunnel through it. Sweat streamed down his face, and the panic built inside him as his young hands beat on the hard surface. But any dent he made was soon filled by a new collapse of snow.

He redoubled his efforts, and Korka bravely joined him, their small hands tearing at the barrier. When they heard a choking noise from the other side, they dug even harder.

They eventually broke through, and Aron tumbled into Jon's hands. Jon hugged him close, so very close, placing his ear above the boy's mouth to make sure Aron was still breathing. His own chest relaxed a little when it felt Aron's rib cage rise and fall.

"He's alive," Jon told Korka. "Let's get out of here!"

That's when the quiet bundle in his arms broke into shrill screaming.

"Shh, shh," Korka said, pulling Aron from Jon's arms.

Jon watched as Aron opened his eyes and gazed into his sister's face. The boy went calm and quiet. But from that day on, he spoke less and avoided tight, dark spaces.

Jon never managed to throw off the yoke of guilt for having been the one to lead them into that cave in the first place. His parents never found out, and he's pretty sure neither Korka nor Aron remember. They were too young, he figures, and they've never mentioned it. If only he could wipe it from his own memory.

Korka is tugging on the edge of his jacket, which yanks Jon back to the present. "The helicopter is gone," she says. We can get out of here now!"

"Aron? You okay?" he asks the quiet boy beside him. Aron is studying him like he's reading Jon's thoughts, a sensation that makes Jon uncomfortable. "You've been dragging a while, Young Viking. Need a rest?"

Aron shakes his head vigorously. But half an hour later, when darkness looms and they make camp, Jon watches his brother pull off a boot and sock and set them in the snow.

"Oh no," Jon says, sitting down beside him after the fire is made, the bathroom hole dug, and supper half-prepared. "You should have told me you were getting a blister. It's a bad one."

Aron winces as Jon examines the puffy red balloon with all the care of an EMT.

"Not popped yet, but just about, and that's when it can get infected. Korka, hand me the first-aid kit."

"*Please*, you tyrant," she says.

"Whatever," he says, watching Aron's eyes focus on the kit Korka hands over. Jon cleans his own hands, applies antiseptic to the blister and area around it, and removes a scalpel blade from a packet in the kit. He lances the wound in two areas and allows it to drain. Aron doesn't even flinch. Then Jon applies more antiseptic and a sterile dressing and deposits the used scalpel in a special container.

"Brave Viking," he tells Aron, who smiles.

"What'd you do that for?" Korka asks, disapproval in her voice.

"Lancing lets the blister dry and heal," Jon replies patiently. "If you don't catch a blister in time and it gets infected, it's as dangerous as an open wound. In other words, it would be the end of our hiding out."

"But why not do it with a thread and needle, like I've heard about?"

"The thread will have bacteria on it, and even a fire-sterilized needle or knife can leave carbon deposits that encourage infection," Jon says. "Better to carry a pre-sterilized scalpel you use only once. I'll have to re-dress the blister maybe twice a day for a week to make sure it's okay. We have moleskin if anyone else feels one coming on."

"Not me," Korka says proudly.

Aron pokes at the roaring campfire. He started it with their steel and flint, even though they have matches they dipped in melted wax before they left, to make them waterproof. Jon observes his apparently unfazed brother and sighs. He's annoyed at himself for not checking on Aron earlier. What kind of leader lets a potential disaster arise so early in the trip?

But he can't bear to think that way. He turns to cooking instead. Tonight he has chosen to make freeze-dried chili, rice, and peas, which everyone is soon digging into. Next, Jon strings a rope between two trees, then hangs the food bag from the middle at just the right height to stop bears and other hungry thieves from reaching it. Finally, they settle into the tent.

"I miss Mom and Dad," Korka says, sniffling. She puts her arms around Aron.

"We all do," Jon says quietly, but he bottles up all the emotion threatening to let loose and orders himself to set an example. Look forward, not back.

So proud of you, son. Keep an eye on your siblings today. Jon plays back his father's words to comfort himself, but his chest seizes.

He recalls the time when he and Mark, aged thirteen, decided to camp on a hillock just above Peakton. The deal was to bring no food, water, or water-purification system and eat only berries along the way. Boneheads that they were, they thought they could clean the water they needed using a sock filtering method. They knotted the top of a sock loosely and suspended it from a branch. Then they poured silty creek water into the top of the sock and caught what dribbled out from the bottom in their metal camping cups.

Barely had they set up the sock when Korka and Aron, ten and seven at the time, burst from some bushes below, shouting, "Surprise! We followed you!"

"What the —?" Mark said, cupping his head in his hands.

"How'd you —? Do Mom and Dad know?" Jon was furious. His eyes moved to their palms, stained black and purple. "Have you been eating berries on the way up?"

"Yup!" Korka asserted proudly. "Just like you."

He unfurled her fists and examined the berries she was still clutching. "No! You didn't eat the same ones as us, Korka! Aron, let me see your hands. Mark! We have to get some water in these guys, and haul them home right away."

The sock got a full workout for the next while, as Korka's and Aron's faces grew green and creased and they placed their hands on their tummies. A vigorous vomit-fest later, the boys hoisted them piggyback style and hauled them down the hill home.

"Never follow us again without telling us, okay?" Jon scolded them.

"Okay," Korka said weakly, her face limp and clammy on his neck.

"White and yellow berries are usually poisonous," Jon instructed them along the way, like his Dad had told him dozens of times. "Half of red berries are poisonous. Blue and black ones are usually okay. Never eat plants that irritate your skin or lips. Chew but don't swallow if you're not sure, and hold them in your mouth for fifteen minutes to check for a reaction. Mark and I know this stuff, and it's about time you did, too. Got it?"

"Got it," Korka mumbled. Aron just groaned.

While Jon and Mark marched down the hill, the younger two subdued and co-operative, their parents ran up to meet them. Later, after the two fugitives were tucked in bed, Jon's father, his face stricken, turned to Jon and Mark and said, "You acted very responsibly today. And the kids recited to me what they learned from you, which is the most important thing, because it means it won't happen again."

Jon still remembers the glow he felt inside at that moment. As he and Mark exchanged glances, he saw it in his buddy, too. They were heroes, champions, saviours, ace rescuers.

"But a sock filter takes out only dirt and vegetation," his father continued, "not waterborne protozoa and bacteria. You can get deadly sick if you're not careful. That's why we have drops, tablets, and filtration and purification devices. Use them next time."

"Yes, Dad."

Must teach them things as we go along, Jon tells himself. There's no telling if the three might get separated, or Jon incapacitated, at some point. "A strong leader creates other leaders," he remembers his father saying.

The ravens that visit at first light fail to wake anyone. Not when one takes the zipper tab of the hanging pack into its beak and tugs it. Not when the packages of food spill to the snowy ground. And not when the invaders proceed to puncture, spill, and eat some of the rations.

Jon hears Korka crawl out of the tent at dawn, probably to go to the toilet hole. "What the —?" she yells, prompting Jon to scramble from the tent. "Get outta here, you devils! Out of here!" She's flapping her arms and clapping her hands. The ravens swoop away, but not far.

Jon sinks into the snow and rakes his hands through his messy hair. "Who'd have thought a raven could unzip a bag?"

"You hung the bag," Korka accuses him. "You're the one who kept telling us how important it was to hang it so bears wouldn't get our food."

"Korka, I've never, ever heard of a raven doing this. Why now? Why to us?"

"Because you don't know everything. You always act like you do, but admit it for once, you don't!"

"How's that helping, you little brat? Stop standing there spouting off and blaming me and get your butt in gear to save what we can."

Aron pokes his head out of the tent, eyes large.

Korka leans down into Jon's face. "Ask like that and *no one*'s going to help clean up *your* mess!"

"Korka, grow up! Can't you see this is urgent? All three of us need to save every single grain, raisin, and nut we can."

"All three of us," Korka mimics in a high voice.

That's when Jon sees tears roll down Aron's face. Aron draws his head back into the tent, which shakes with the sobs he's probably trying hard to stop but can't.

"Now see what you've done?" Jon's rage erupts within his chest and he jabs a finger at Korka. "Like I'm going to let you have any supper tonight if you don't help! Or maybe we'll just leave you behind if you can't be a team player!"

She freezes as Aron's snuffling escalates into wailing. As they stand over the mess, Jon can tell she's clearly torn between entering the tent to comfort her brother and continuing the fight. Instead of doing either, she turns and focuses her fury on a returning raven. "Get, or we'll kill you for dinner!" she screeches. "You horrible, thieving scoundrels! I hate you! I hate you!" The tears stream down her face.

This is not about the ravens, Jon realizes too late, breathing deeply to steady himself. This is grief leaching out, grief they've all packed away, deep, deep in their raw souls, attempting to encase it in an impermeable container. The loss they've suffered is too big, too overwhelming, too flammable to risk exposing to oxygen. They must keep it locked inside them until they're safe, or there will be no energy to survive.

Korka falls to her knees and begins collecting anything that's still edible. "Thank you, Korka," Jon says. The tent goes still and quiet.

"Lucky I found it before it brought around a bigger animal," she says, glancing into the woods.

"True," Jon says.

"I'll slay the invaders with my slingshot," says a voice from the tent. Aron crawls out. He wipes his puffy face with one arm and narrows his eyes at a raven that's still watching sulkily from a nearby perch.

"I know you could, Young Viking, but how about we rescue all the food we can first?" Jon suggests gently, cupping Aron's head in his hands.

Soon the only sounds are the crunch of knees working their way through frozen grass and bits of food plopping into tin cups.

Jon tries to breathe away the knot in his gut. "They've stolen more than a week's worth of food from us. We had enough for a month without much hunting, fishing, and gathering. It's serious, but it doesn't put us in immediate danger. It does mean we'll have to fish and snare before I thought we would, and eat less than we'd like."

Aron holds up his slingshot. "Young Viking will serve blue grouse stuffed with berries for supper tonight."

Blue grouse are the meatiest of the grouse, but they live at higher elevations. Berries aren't going to be on the menu for months. Not that Jon is going to point that out to Aron, especially in his fragile state.

"Okay, counting on you, Aron," Jon says. But what he thinks is this: *At all costs, we are not turning back.*

TEN

They settle into a routine that satisfies Jon. Early each morning, he lowers the food bag, starts the camp stove (to avoid campfire smoke that might alert searchers), and makes a thick porridge before waking his siblings. After breakfast, Korka melts ice or snow to wash the dishes and fill their water bottles with water she carefully purifies. Or she occasionally finds a stream with water beneath a crust of ice for these jobs. Aron packs the sleeping bags and gear and helps Jon take down and stow the tent. Before they leave camp, they use twigs to brush the campsite to hide all signs — they hope — of habitation. Then they're off to see how many kilometres they can put in before it's time to pause for lunch. All the better if it's a lunch spot with a viewpoint, showing endless valleys, trees, and snow-iced mountains marching into a lavender sky.

"What's for lunch?" Aron always asks.

"PB and J," Korka always answers.

The never-varying exchange starts as a sarcastic joke, turns annoying, then becomes a giggle session for the two of them. Whatever floats their boat, Jon reasons. Laughter counters stress. Laughter camouflages layers of black grief and trauma no one can afford to admit to in these marathon marches, which are saturated with a fear of searchers, hunters, and fellow hikers and punctuated periodically by planes overhead. Their feet and calves harden up. Their sixth sense for approaching planes and people excels. Their nerves never rest.

By evening, they're looking for a camping spot flat enough for their tent, near a water source if possible, and far enough off the trail to thwart followers. Once they've chosen, Jon produces the trowel and digs a toilet site, getting faster at it every day. Aron wordlessly erects the tent and unpacks the sleeping bags, while Jon and Korka collect firewood if they've deemed it safe to risk a little smoke. After all, they dare not use up all their stove fuel early on. Aron continually beats his own record in fire starting, and Jon declares what's for supper. After they eat, Jon hangs the food bag, Aron often helping just so he can perform antics on the high rope for a while.

"Upside down now!" Korka eggs him on. "Okay, how far can you swing out before you jump?"

"Don't encourage him to injure himself," Jon objects.

"What are you, an old, grumpy grandpa?" she retorts.

Days into their journey, they're making their way along the edge of some dense woods when Korka hears muffled voices that seem to come from just over a nearby ridge. Or is it merely the trickle of a stream in the forest?

She can see no one, but she shushes the others with a finger over her mouth, then elbows her way quickly into an extra dense section of trees.

Aron and Jon follow and drop to their stomachs. Korka sees two men crest the ridge just seconds later, only a stone's throw from their hiding spot. The men would have caught the three of them for sure if they hadn't been talking, or if Korka's ears weren't so sharp. She watches Jon lift the binoculars to his eyes. His face tightens. It's the third time they've hidden from helicopters and people, but these men are way closer than previous ground crews have been. Almost close enough to smell.

"Hikers?" she whispers.

"Or searchers?" Aron asks.

"You just saved us, Korka," Jon admits. "Now, shhh. Don't move. Don't breathe."

Kind of hard to exist long without breathing, Korka wants to remind him.

"Won't last long. Could be in bad shape already," one man is saying.

"More experience than most," the other replies. "I have hope we'll find them alive."

"Tragic," says the first man. "So unnecessary to run like that." The two pause and do a slow rotation with their binoculars. They stare into the woods like they're trying to figure out whether and where to enter. Korka tries to give Aron a reassuring look. He's shivering, and even something so little as a cracked twig might alert the men to their presence.

"They thought they were pretty clever, leaving their truck by the bus station. Like authorities wouldn't check surveillance cameras and figure out they never boarded. But certainly makes the search difficult, having no idea where ..."

The voices fade as the men carry on parallel to the woods, then disappear back over the ridge. Korka feels her joints tighten with the cold and fear. Will they double back? Are there more behind them? Are they professional trackers and have they found signs of them already? Will the next team have sniffer dogs or night-vision goggles?

"How many days do you think people will search?" she whispers to Jon, then wishes she hadn't, since that implies he knows anything more than she does.

He sighs. "We're kids. They won't call off a search for a long time." Then he points up at the sky, and sure enough, a helicopter they've seen before slowly passes overhead, rotates, and *thwaks* back, disturbing the peace of the woods and any peace of mind Korka has sought desperately the past few days.

"We're kids, but we're as sharp as them," she declares. "They won't catch us."

"Yeah," Aron chimes in, and she hugs him, if only to counter her own body's shivers.

Aron is disappointed that they don't gain a lot of mileage the following week, given the stealth with which they have to proceed. They encounter one more party of evil searchers, this one quieter and more diligent than the first, but not stalwart enough to lay siege to them as they pull sticks over themselves in a gully. But as soon as the coast is clear and they've departed the gully, Aron steps in some defecation.

"Eeew," he says. "Fresh." And so noxious.

Jon leans down and examines the mess clogging the soles of Aron's boots.

"Bear scat. Grizzly. Really, really fresh," he notes. His head turns this way and that, and a bead of sweat appears on his forehead.

Aron feels his heartbeat triple, and he looks for a tree he can spring up if the malicious beast dares to show. This Viking does not want to be part of a banquet, nor does he want his fellow clan members to be compromised by his lesser tree-climbing prowess. Especially if persistent pursuers might hear their cries or see them high in the trees.

He knows the leader and maiden have been silently frustrated with his much-limited progress of late, although diplomatic enough not to comment upon it. Despite the Nordic deities giving him the strength to get this far and sparing the three from being found in the gully, he feels the heat of the enemies' torches, the fieriness of the hovering beast's breath, the sultriness of their situation. The calefaction of —

"Aron? Aron, are you okay?" Jon is leaning over him, which must mean he has collapsed onto the ground. It should be cold, but it's strangely sweltering. He's hot, so very hot, and Jon's hand on his forehead is welcomingly cool.

"I need a … a … potion," he says as the sky darkens, drops down, and presses firmly on his eyelids.

"He's feverish," Jon is saying to Korka, but their voices are miles away. "Why didn't he say anything? And how did I not suspect he was ill before now? Grab the bear spray and stand guard while I find the thermometer and some acetaminophen in the medical kit. We're going to camp here. Yes, right here, bear close by or not."

"I could shout and get the searchers' attention," Korka says meekly.

Through his haze, Aron notes that Jon hesitates for a split second, but no longer than that. "No. We can handle this."

The fever lasts a worrying three days, during which Jon hovers over his quivering, sweating brother. It's difficult to persuade Aron to eat anything, but Korka manages to get some soup down him once or twice, which Jon appreciates. The EMT in him diagnoses a sinus infection. The brother in him is on the edge of freaking out. He monitors Aron around the clock, pushing fluids, frowning

over a rapid heart rate, giving him medicine for his head-
aches and temperature.

When the fever breaks at the end of the third day —
which Jon knows is the longest a fever should last without
a doctor's attention — Aron remains weak and drowsy.
So, they continue to stay in their gully-side camp, taking
extra care when they hang the diminishing food bag to
keep wildlife away, and securing the zippers with duct
tape to outwit any smartass ravens.

"I'm cold. Can I start a fire?" Korka asks.

"Only with a water container nearby in case Search
and Rescue gets anywhere close. Even then the smoke
could identify us."

"I know, but we can't just freeze here for fear of them.
And there are fewer airplanes and helicopters lately." She
sighs. "I miss Aron's fire-starting abilities," she adds as
she starts to build a pyramid of shavings and twigs. But
Jon is relieved she manages to get the fire going without
using up too many matches.

A few nights later, Jon awakens to the crunch of footsteps outside the tent. Heart pounding against his ribs, he
reaches for his headlamp, but fights the panic that urges
him to switch it on immediately. The person or thing is rust-
ling around their campsite. He can't judge if it's one human
being, or creature, or more. His throat closes up when the
noise stops for a long period, then starts again. Searching silently in the dark for his knife, and reminding himself to be
more consistent about keeping it under his rolled-up-jeans
pillow at night, he slithers out of his sleeping bag and unzips
the tent door so slowly that no one could possibly hear.

"Jon?" comes Korka's sleepy voice. Okay, no one except Korka.

"Shhh." And that exchange is all it takes for all hell to break loose in their campsite, a thunder of steps and a bump against the tent that sends his pulse rate soaring.

He switches on the headlamp and aims it in every direction, like it's a pistol in a trench that's being overrun by enemy soldiers. The white rumps of retreating bodies finally notify him that a few harmless deer have been sniffing around.

Korka yawns beside him. "They were cute. But I'd eat all of them in one meal if I had the option. G'night Jon."

So true, Jon thinks, his hungry stomach cramping at the very mention of food. They must move ahead as soon as Aron's ready and do better at catching game in the meantime. He tells himself it will get easier as spring warms the mountain valleys. He rises to do a thorough check of the campsite and food bag, which is swaying gently overhead in the breeze like a slow-motion pendulum. It's undisturbed, out of reach of bears and its ropes too icy for even a tightrope-walking champ of a weasel to try.

ELEVEN

Many mornings later — Jon has given up keeping track of time — and many kilometres farther along, he sets out to check on a snare he set the evening before. Their need to catch food to supplement their fast-dwindling supplies is becoming critical. Not yet a matter of life or death, but the hungrier and weaker hikers get, the more mistakes they're likely to make, and one error bringing on another can be a very dangerous downward spiral. It's a notion that has jumped from being part of a lecture in his parents' survival classes to now overshadowing Jon's everyday life. His greatest fear is running out of food when they're far from anywhere. It takes a lot of calories for three people to stay on the move in the cold. He simply must find something in his snare today.

As he creeps close to where he laid the snare between small trees, he finds himself crossing his numb fingers for luck. His is a small-game snare, a wire circle hung a few centimetres over an animal trail and anchored to thicker wire that he's wrapped around a tree. Larger, stronger snares can catch coyotes, wolves, fox, beavers, even wild boars in other regions, but his is more likely to capture a rabbit or squirrel. You'd have to be desperate to eat fox meat, anyway, he has heard, and he has no idea what a beaver would taste like. But anything with meat on it would please him today. He has not yet caught anything on this journey, as Korka is quick to remind him. It makes him angry and tense. What could he be doing wrong?

Relax. The snare will feed us this time, he tells himself.

He can see it up ahead, and he swears he can make out a shadow within it and smell fresh blood. Nothing's moving. He hopes it's a fresh catch that didn't suffer long.

Moving faster now, he ducks under branches and makes a beeline for the hump of whatever it is in his snare. "Noooo!" he hollers so loudly that snow spills down from branches above. "Noooo!" Then he chokes off the cry, remembering there could be searchers within hearing distance at any time.

He stamps his feet, curses, and grabs the snare, emptying it of the mostly eaten squirrel. In one angry swoop, he sends the carcass flying through the air. "Who ate our lunch?" he growls. A coyote? Weasel? Marten? Owl?

Raven? No, given the tiny claw prints on the trail, the thief was a crow. "Hope you enjoyed it. Next time I'll eat *you*," he threatens the branches above him, shaking his raised fist.

But wait! His snare worked! The anchor was sufficiently secure, and he'd known to place it in the two-o'clock position and over a well-defined trail. It had worked. He just hadn't been there to nab it before an experienced squirrel-snatcher did.

"Survival of the fittest," he mumbles. "Next time I'll stay up all night if I have to. I'm not here to feed scavengers, you filthy bandits. Next time the catch will be mine!"

"Nothing?" Korka greets him, seeing the snare hanging loosely from his limp hand.

He doesn't look at her or try to alter his long face. He just braces for whatever nasty comment she's going to make next.

"You got something," she says, pointing at bits of flesh and fur still clinging to the wire.

"A crow beat me to it," he says, staring at the ground and wishing it would swallow him up.

"But it worked," she says in an upbeat tone that doesn't sound entirely forced. "So it will again. Sorry you lost it this time," she finishes sadly, and almost kindly.

"Thanks. Aron up yet?"

"Taking a piss."

"Language." Like he really cares. Like even Mom and Dad would at this point. Aron has fully recovered from his sinus infection and fever and has finally regained his strength. He's been rising ever earlier these days, which means maybe they can get a good start this morning. But — Jon's jaw drops when he sees Aron sprinting toward the tent from the woods, a finger pressed to his lips, face fully animated. *Uh-oh. What's up?*

"Follow me!" Aron whispers urgently.

They let the youngest lead them to a frosty, tree-shaded hillock a five-minute walk from their tent. Jon brings his pack with him, and touches the knife on his belt to reassure himself it's there. When Aron drops to the ground, Jon and Korka follow suit without questioning, like they're a trio of soldiers on reconnaissance. Jon feels the chill on his stomach as he lies on the rise between his siblings. From under the canopy of swaying branches, they peer out on a morning-lit clearing, dazzling white. An iced-over stream snakes down the middle of the large snowy meadow. At the far end, half in the trees, stands a black dot. The dot is moving.

Slowly, the dark figure grows as it lumbers toward the stream. It resembles a hunchback horse.

"A moose," Korka exclaims.

"It's female, 'cause it doesn't have antlers, right?" Aron asks Jon.

Jon's watching the creature. Something is wrong in the way it's moving. He searches his pack for their binoculars. "Males shed their antlers in early winter," he says distract-edly, "and don't grow them back till spring, so it could be either. But I'd lay my money on male, given the size of it. That's like fifteen hundred pounds walking toward us."

"They don't hibernate," Korka says proudly, like she's some kind of moose expert.

"If they don't hibernate, what do they eat this time of year?" Aron asks his sister.

Korka is quick to answer. "Bark and twigs."

Not far off what we're going to be forced to eat soon, Jon thinks miserably.

"The word *moose* actually means 'twig eater' in an Algonquin language," Korka continues. "And they're way dangerous because they can charge at like fifty-five kilometres an hour, so don't talk so loud, Aron."

Jon smiles at this, given how far away the moose is. "They don't usually charge except during fall mating season, or in spring when calves come," he reassures her. "We're in between those times, and I'm thinking this guy's an old grandpa on his own." An old grandpa who seems multicoloured, which is very strange. A mottled moose?

The three go quiet as the moose nears the stream, still a great distance from them. Jon fiddles with the binocular knobs to focus in on him. "Moose burgers would be nice," he says, knowing they have no weapons that could take it down, but hearing his stomach rumbling, anyway.

As the moose arrives at the frozen creek, the binoculars reveal a sad-looking, shaggy specimen. His spindly legs, the lower halves white like he's wearing knee socks, support an emaciated beast with uneven fur patches. His horse-like nostrils are emitting laboured puffs of breath visible in the cold, and his chest seems to heave with the effort. His beard — the flap of skin beneath his

PAM WITHERS

throat — looks kind of moth-eaten, and his large ears are twitching as if on high alert.

"I didn't know moose could be white," Aron whispers. "Not all white, but white and brown at the same time."

"He's a ghost moose," Jon informs them.

"You mean like a spirit bear?" Korka asks with enthusiasm. "Or an albino?"

"No, the poor thing is infested with so many moose ticks that he rubs hard on trees to try to get rid of them. That takes patches of his hair off, which makes it hard for him to survive winter temperatures, even if the ticks haven't made him anemic. Ghost moose aren't a new thing, but climate change is making them more common, Dad told me. Milder winters don't kill off the moose ticks like winters used to."

"Gimme the binoculars!" Aron says in a loud whisper. "There's something following him."

That prompts grabbing and tugging from Korka and Aron, but Jon is quick to hand them over to his brother once he confirms there is indeed a wolf following Grandpa Moose. That has to be why Grandpa Moose's ears stiffen and jerk forward and his nostrils flare.

Jon knows instantly what's about to unfold, and what their part in it must be. "Aron, Korka!" he commands as he plunges his hands into his pack for matches and tinder. "We need to start a fire. Immediately! Grab some kindling and dry wood from around here. And three long sticks."

"Stop bossing!" Korka starts in.

"I'm watching the moose!" Aron insists, binoculars pressed against his face.

"Now! Fast as you can! Life or death!" Jon all but bellows. He has already set up a tinder teepee and is blowing on the first curl of smoke that emerges from it.

Apparently alarmed by his tone, Korka and Aron spring into action, well practised by now at speed-gathering kindling and firewood. The fire takes by the time the wolf draws abreast of the moose, who is attempting to gallop away. It's starting to crackle by the time the wolf lunges for the moose's forward left armpit and holds on for dear life, apparently unfazed by the moose's swerving and bucking. It's a healthy little fire by the time a second and third wolf join the scene.

"Oh!" Korka exclaims as the moose manages to send one wolf flying with a kick from his back hoof. But the wolf rolls in the snow and leaps up again, and when it catches up, it sinks its teeth into the moose's behind.

"Wolves are killing machines," Korka mumbles, hands covering her mouth.

"Not true. The wolves are just trying to live," Jon says. "And Dad said they get only one moose in every twelve they try to kill. Plus, it's a faster, less painful way for an old moose to die than from old age. Wolves are an important part of nature."

"He's bleeding! He's stumbling," Aron says in a flat, sorrowful voice.

"Three large sticks, Korka, please," Jon urges.

Hardly tearing her eyes off the Nature-Channel-gone-live scene in front of her, Korka finds three long sticks and drags them back to their site within minutes.

"Is the fire to protect us?" she asks, trembling slightly as the moose goes down, then struggles up, the wolves tearing at him all the time. "Are the wolves going to kill us next?"

"Wolves don't attack people," Jon says. "Not even if we steal their kill, as long as we have fire sticks." Jon thrusts the tips of the sticks into the fire.

His siblings stare at him as the moose falters and plunges into the snow again, kicking madly at the wolves pouncing on him. The snow under the moose begins to turn red.

"Now!" Jon orders, picking up one of the long sticks and raising its flaming end like a torch. With his other hand, he grabs the cold bone handle of his hunting knife. Though his insides are shaking, he lifts his face, squints his eyes, and juts out his chin in an attempt to look fearless, so that his siblings will follow suit. A wolf's strongest sense is smell, and it can smell fear.

Korka and Aron exchange looks, then pick up the other two flaming sticks.

Jon grabs a clean T-shirt from his pack and pushes it into his rear waistband before marching straight for the bloody scene, with Korka and Aron following him. The wolves snarl but back up as he gets closer. The moose is still kicking a little.

"Arrghh!" he shouts at the wolves, shaking his fire stick at them.

Later, Korka will ask, "What kind of sound was that? You thought you were a pirate?" But now the wolves scurry off their prize to the edge of the meadow. It's three wolves against three humans, with the fire sticks and human aggression being the deciding factors in who wins.

The moose's patchy skin looks super nasty close up: clusters of swollen ticks cling to it like small pebbles or piles of lentils, some as large as grapes. So gross. The moose smells earthy.

"Okay, keep the wolves away!" Jon instructs Korka and Aron.

"L-like h-how?" Aron asks. But he follows Korka's lead as she positions herself behind the dying moose and throws fierce looks at the wolves, pointing both her stick and Jon's at them like she's a javelin thrower. The resentful wolves, for their part, are keeping a respectful distance. To Jon, they resemble his Peakton neighbours' friendly Alaskan malamutes, who were always eager for a cuddle.

Jon slits the moose's throat quickly, out of mercy. Then, like he learned in one of his father's classes, he grabs hold of the wolf-torn guts, apparently filled with a mass of un-digested twigs, and wrestles all twenty-some kilograms of it out of the animal. Like an erupted outhouse, it emits a smell vile enough to make him to gag. It's beyond foul or fetid. It's so chokingly disgusting that he heaves, but he's determined not to throw up in front of his brother and sister. And he's extremely careful not to let one of the moose's four stomachs rupture as the smelly mess pours into the snow, since that would contaminate the meat.

Next, he uses his knife to skin the animal over the ribs. He does a sloppy job that his father would frown on, but it allows him to proceed to the most important step: re-moving cone-shaped portions of meat, which fall almost neatly into his hands as his fingers and knife follow the natural tissue lines around the bones. He works close to the loin, up toward the spine, then toward the hind. All while keeping half an eye on the waiting wolves and his shivering siblings.

He steps over to the stream and breaks its ice to wash blood and dirt from each precious, steaming meat cone, while also cooling them. Then he pulls the clean T-shirt out of his waistband and wraps the pieces and a slice of fat in it. Finally, he nods at Korka and Aron, and they all return to their rise and his pack, Jon staggering under the weight of the precious meat. They douse the little stick fire and head for their campsite. Jon turns twice to check where the wolves are. His spear-bearers guard his rear the whole way, walking backward, less trusting than he is that the wolves will stay put.

A third glance back reveals the wolves, a wary species, still waiting to return to their kill. They're looking about, sniffing, glancing over their shoulders at the interlopers. But eventually they sense it's safe and lope over to the moose. They shove their muzzles into the carcass, tearing at the remaining meat with sharp incisors, gulping with gusto.

"Plenty of meat still for them," Jon says. He sways slightly as adrenalin is replaced by acute tiredness — and triumph.

"We have moose meat," Korka says, wonder in her tone. "Now what?"

"They let us have it," Aron half whispers, like generosity was involved.

"I couldn't have done it without you," Jon says, staring at what he guesses is almost fifteen kilograms of steak in front of him, his heart still pounding against his ribs.

"But what about the moose's horrible skin, the ticks?" Korka asks, making a face. "Doesn't that make the meat bad?"

"Nope," says Jon, pleased he remembers this from his course. "So, grab some more firewood and let's get started, team. It's going to take all day to make jerky and pemmican."

"Remind me the difference?" Korka asks.

"Jerky is strips of meat dried in the sun. It tastes good. Pemmican is dried meat ground into powder and mixed with fat and berries to make a flat patty that's pretty tasteless."

"Why not just do jerky, then?" Aron asks.

"Because pemmican lasts longer."

And so they slice the meat thinly and place it on hand-made stick racks. Some pieces rest in the sun till Jon rules it jerky, and others dry slowly over the fire till the meat is crispy as bacon. There are no blueberries around yet, but they dump the finely crumbled meat into boiling fat with a bit of sugar, then press the mix into locking plastic bags, flatten them to remove as much air as possible, and declare them moose burgers.

"How long does pemmican last?" Aron asks.

"Years if you do it right," Jon says, "but with three active Vikings, we'll be lucky if this batch lasts more than a week."

Still, they're definitely able to feast for the next while on the protein their bodies so crave, first on the fresh meat, then on the jerky, and finally on the pemmican, which Korka rules "totally, seriously gross."

TWELVE

Jon guesses they've been in the mountains more than a month now, and the springlike air confirms it. He breathes it in like a tonic as he stands behind Aron, who is slumped on a stump, dirty and sunburned, and looking for all the world like an aged gnome. Jon flips the greasy, matted hair out of his brother's eyes and presses his hunting knife to the bangs. It's not like there are any barber shops on this wilderness journey, and all three of them are beginning to look like wild animals. To feel like them, too, with shrunken, rumbling bellies, worn boots, the occasional tear in their clothes, and a constant alertness to forest sounds.

They're still a few days from the mining town, delayed by Aron's fever and the need to avoid hiking parties or searchers several times. Between the ravens and the weeks on the trail, and despite the moose-meat bounty now eaten up, they're down to less than one-quarter of their food, less than a week's supply unless they find stuff to eat.

A nearby pink pine grosbeak treats them to a flute-like warble, and Aron cocks his head toward it.

"Stop moving," Jon says, knife poised above his brother's rat's-nest of hair.

"Don't cut too much," Korka directs from another stump, twigs tangled in her own braids. "Just enough so he can see."

At the whine of a small plane overhead, Jon whips his knife back into its sheath and scrambles into thick brush. The others follow and land on top of him.

"Never gonna get us!" Korka shouts upward, raising a fist.

The plane flies off and doesn't backtrack. It has been days since they've seen one, Jon reminds himself, so it might not even be searching for them.

He unsheathes his hunting knife again, this time to pierce an extra hole in his leather belt, which no longer holds up his filthy jeans.

"Getting fashionably skinny?" Korka asks dully.

"Mmm."

She steps to a nearby tree, peers up into it, and applies her muscled arms and legs to it. Up she climbs, high into the branches, until she is within hand's reach of a bird's nest. An old bird's nest, Jon could tell her, given the time of year, but he doesn't want to dampen her enthusiasm.

Legs wrapped around the branch, Korka leans perilously out to peer into the nest. She says a bad word, another thing Jon won't bother commenting on.

"Too early in the season for eggs," he suggests gently, "but proud of you for trying, Korka."

"Proud of you for trying," she mimics, her tone sassy, and scrabbles down the tree so fast he isn't sure she hasn't fallen.

"You okay?" he asks.

"No. Starving," she retorts.

Despite the moose meat and the occasional caught bird or fish, all three of them are thinner and slower moving than when they set out. In fact, they've carefully rationed what they have left. Worse, the stove fuel is almost gone, and they have days to go before they reach the mining town. No wonder they're dragging, Jon reflects.

"Okay, sit up on the stump again?" Jon directs Aron in as jolly a voice as he can manage.

Aron leans back into the bush with arms crossed like he's on a sit-down strike. His face is pale and his walking has been a little shaky this afternoon.

"A blister again?" Jon asks, frowning, still annoyed with himself for missing the first one until it needed medical attention. "Sinuses okay? No fever, right?"

Aron shakes his head. He grimaces, holding up his empty water bottle and placing one hand on his stomach.

Jon's heart contracts. In trying to speed up their mileage today, he has been leading them along a windswept, snowless ridge that has offered little in the way of water. He failed to pause and suggest water-bottle refills even when they could have punched through the ice over a streamlet. Both Korka's and Aron's water bottles are empty.

He's a bad leader. He's losing it.

Korka turns weary eyes and sunken cheeks toward him. "Death occurs in three minutes without oxygen," she quotes a wilderness manual, "three hours without shelter in a storm, three days without water, and three weeks without food."

"Uh-huh," Jon responds.

"At least we have oxygen." Her sarcasm drips like springtime tree sap.

"Korka, you're not helping. Aron, do you feel dizzy?" Jon crouches in front of his brother and feels his forehead to make sure the fever hasn't crept back. "Have any tingling in the arms and legs?"

That's stage two of dehydration, before a swollen tongue and deafness set in. They're already in stage one for sure: irritability, nausea, and weakness. Irritability being Korka's default state lately.

Aron shakes his head no. Jon passes him his own bottle and watches him drain its last few drops. Then Jon rises and scans the valley down the ridge, knowing there's plenty of water down there, under thin ice or not. He curses himself again for dragging them up here. His intention was to save a little time, and to stay off the main trail in case anyone's still searching for them. But the cost has been too great.

Jon turns back to his sister. "Korka, are you okay?"

"I would be if we were at home watching TV, guzzling soda, and stuffing down grilled cheese sandwiches. Are we lost, by the way? Maybe you should let me do the map reading."

"We're not lost. You guys want to rest here? I can take a shortcut down that gully and bring back some water," he says, although his own thirst and hunger are making him a bit dizzy.

No reply. Just exhausted-looking faces.

"Never mind. We'll all go. We need to stick together." He places reassuring hands on both their heads. He'll pursue the haircut later. "I'm sorry the snare hasn't caught us as much food as I was hoping. And that I've been pushing us so hard. But we should hit the ghost town in a few days. Peakton's way behind us now." Not that he'd turn back.

"A few days ..." Korka moans dramatically.

Aron stiffens and points down the gully at the dense, snowy forest beyond it.

"What?" Jon asks.

"I smell smoke."

Jon sniffs hard and scans the area with the binoculars, but he sees and smells nothing. Searchers? Not likely. Hikers? Maybe. Hunters? That wouldn't be good. He has been afraid all along of people with guns out there scanning for movement. He sees nothing. Aron has always had a super sensitive nose, but then again, maybe this is just his imagination.

"Do you see it, or just smell it?" he asks.

Aron points to his nose.

"See or smell anything, Korka? I don't." At least it's not hunting season, he reminds himself.

"Nope," she says, studying Aron.

Aron purses his lips and squints at the valley.

"Okay," Jon says, "we're going to make our way to that ledge over there, then down the scree slope till we're in that hollow in the white spruce trees. We'll have to be careful of the sharp rocks as we climb down. That's where we'll find water, even if we have to chip ice to get to it. We need to stop using precious fuel to boil snow. Be careful. We all have to hold hands and stay together."

"*Have* to? Not *me*," says Korka, crossing her arms.

"Korka, this is about safety," Jon says. "And you need to set an example for Aron." *Why is she always so difficult?*

"Maybe I'll decide what's safe. And how about you take him for once? What's for supper when we set up camp down there, anyway?"

"Grouse stuffed with berries," Aron promises them for the umpteenth time, hand on his slingshot. Jon could swear Aron believes it every time.

"Oh, stuff it, Aron," Korka barks.

"Korka —"

"And you shut up, too. You're the reason we're lost and starving. Mom and Dad would know what to do."

A pain shoots through Jon's chest. "We're not —" He stops himself. They're all exhausted, sleep-deprived, wrapped in grief, and running on empty. But they're still together. His own patience is wearing thin, but he won't show it. He has to make sure they keep a lid on things for a little while longer. Why is Korka such a rebel? How did Mom and Dad handle her? *Mom, Dad, help me! Help us!*

His memory drifts back to a time when Mom grounded Korka. When Korka and a friend learned that a group of boys wouldn't allow girls to play hockey with them on a local pond, they decided action was called for. They boiled up water in very large pots early one Saturday morning and lugged them out there one by one to spread on the rink, thinning it without creating obvious holes.

The first boy to hit the ice a short while later fell through, and the other boys didn't know what to do. Korka calmly shouted directions, telling them to feed a board across the surface to rescue him without breaking through the thin ice and contracting hypothermia themselves. But later, someone reported that they'd seen Korka, her friend, and their steaming pots.

"I understand you were upset about being left out, but deliberately putting people's lives at risk is unacceptable. I'd never have thought you capable of that, Korka," their mother had said, her voice quavering with anger and humiliation.

The boy was fine, but his mother wouldn't speak to the Gunnarssons for weeks. Korka and her friend were grounded for a week and banned from skating for even longer. Mom and Dad ordered Korka to stay in her room except during school hours and mealtimes. She considered the punishment so outrageous that she loudly declared a hunger strike and refused to come downstairs for meals.

It wasn't exactly a full-on act of protest, since she asked Jon to sneak food up to her room at night. Their parents definitely worried about her, though, until they found some of the telltale crumbs. Jon smiles at the memory.

He wishes that recalling this might give him a clue as to how to handle her now. But it doesn't. He shakes himself out of his memory and sighs. He wants to sink to the ground and cover his face with his hands, but he can't do it with his two siblings looking at him. The burden of leading, the acute fear of failure, the hunger and long days of walking — all this is grinding him into the ground. Never mind the galaxy-sized hole in his heart from losing his parents.

Fed up with Korka, fearful that he'll explode on her one of these days and tear apart the fabric of their sworn threesome, he looks to Aron. The slingshot sticking out of his little brother's torn pocket reminds him of the one thing he and Korka seem to agree on: Their brother's hunting skills are nothing to bank on. Then again, Jon is equally frustrated by how little he himself has caught in their snare. Maybe it's too early in the season. Spring weather seems to be unusually late, and their need for more than their limited stash of freeze-dried food is taunting. His raw stomach rumbles at the very thought of fresh meat.

"Let's go," he tells the others, pointing to the scree slope. "Remember, be careful." He grips Aron's hand tightly and reaches for Korka's.

She shrugs off his outstretched arm and ploughs ahead. Crap.

Moments later, Jon hears a shrill *fweet*. His head jerks up. A tin whistle. An emergency!

THIRTEEN

Jon imagines rocks crashing down somewhere ahead of Aron and him.

"Korka?" He tells Aron to sit on a safe boulder and picks his way down the slope to see his sister on the ground. Tears slide down her bloodied face and she's gripping her ankle.

Aron climbs down gingerly to join them.

"I told you to hold hands, but no, you had to do things your own way, huh? Now what?" Jon tries to tame the anger in his voice as he touches the scrapes on her face. *Okay, drop the attitude, Jon. Not helping.* Dad would never say anything like that. Jon switches from angry leader to helpful EMT. "Is your head okay? What hurts besides the ankle?"

"Nothing." But she's sobbing.

"Does the ankle hurt when I touch it?" *Gentler voice, Jon. Now you've made her cry. Girls!*

"Yes!" she screams, and Aron rushes to hold her hand.

If he hadn't *ordered* that they hold hands, Jon ponders, maybe she would've been more willing.

"I'd give anything right now to be home, not traipsing around here, cold and hungry and filthy and injured, all because you're such a jerk." Korka sobs.

"It might just be sprained," Jon says, more gently now. *Please don't let it be broken.* It takes at least four weeks for a sprained ankle to heal, he recalls. A broken ankle would be a bigger catastrophe. "When you're ready, test it so we know whether you can put any weight on it."

Bravely, she stops sniffling, grabs at a boulder with both hands, and tries to pull herself up. But she sinks down and shakes her head.

Aron digs out the medical kit, opens it, and offers his sister ibuprofen. The kid's taut face all but begs Jon and Korka not to fight.

"Thanks, Aron," Jon says. "Korka, you'll have to swallow it without water, since we've run out."

She looks at him like it's all his fault. "How about 'Korka, I'm so sorry. Do you think you can swallow a pill without water, since we've run out? I know you can, brave girl.' That's what Mom would've said."

He sighs. She stuffs the tablet into her mouth and gags, but succeeds in getting it down.

"Was there a noise like a bone breaking?" Jon asks. "It's swelling, but it's not a weird shape, which would mean a fracture. Is the pain here?" He probes gently. "Or directly over your ankle bone?"

"Don't!" she cries out, as he rests a finger on the soft part of her ankle.

Okay, probably sprained, Jon thinks with relief.

Aron grabs both Korka's and Jon's packs and hangs one off each shoulder, his own occupying his back. He jabs his thumb at the snow-dusted trees below.

"What, you think you can carry all the packs while I piggyback her?" Jon is incredulous.

Aron nods vigorously, defiantly, staggering forward with a proud smile.

Never underestimate Aron.

"For a little way, anyway," Jon agrees, grateful. "If they get too heavy, take one off and we'll come back for it. But keep holding my hand, Aron." As if his brother would ever do otherwise, being the one sibling who actually obeys. "When you're ready, Korka."

It's almost dark by the time they reach a stream with ice along its edges. Aron lets go of Jon's hand, drops the packs, and heads to the water. He cups it in his palms and begins gulping even before Jon can grab their package of purification tablets from his pack's shoulder strap.

"Aron!" he shouts. "You know that isn't safe! You know the rules."

Aron gives him the finger, marches a few steps into the forest, and hides behind a tree, clearly taunting him. Jon sighs, irritated but resigned. He busies himself purifying water and setting up camp. Maybe Aron needs a little down time. He won't go out of sight, Jon knows. The boy will keep his eyes locked on the two of them from behind his tree. But his defiance, like Korka's, is growing. How can Jon protect them both if one wanders off?

The whole trip is starting to feel like a two-hundred-pound pack, and a part of him wants someone, anyone, to take over. Maybe it was a terrible idea from the beginning. One of them could suffer serious injury at any time, and it'd be all his fault. But they're too far in now — he's it, and they need to survive. Which they can't do without him.

"Korka, you can boil water, right?"

She glares at him for no good reason.

"Okay, Aron," he calls out. "I'll set up the toilet place and pitch the tent for you and get the food out of the pack." Like there's any food worth unpacking.

He heaves a heavy sigh. They need to reach the clutch of houses they're going to call home, set up a routine Korka doesn't fight about, then hike to that store to buy stuff, hopefully without being recognized if there's a missing-persons alert out for them. He touches the bump in his pack that confirms the cash can they brought is still there. If they don't eat something soon, they're going to get light-headed and even more agitated at each other — or worse.

He fetches cold water from the stream and places it in a self-sealing plastic bag against Korka's ankle to hold down the swelling. "No, Korka, hold it more like this," he directs her.

"You think I don't know how to hold a bag?"

Next, he heats a rock in the campfire, winds a T-shirt around it, then wraps the shirt around her elevated limb to alternate heat with the cold. "You need to prop it up to keep the swelling down."

"Like I wouldn't know that. Want to tell me exactly what angle I need to prop it at, micromanager?"

He can't believe she even knows that word. It raises his hackles crazy high. "You should've stayed with us like I told you to. If —"

"If you stopped treating us like little kids and said thank you once in a while for all the chores you order us to do —"

"I'm trying to get you to safety!" he roars. "And to food!"

"Yeah, and where's the food, then, fearless self-appointed leader?" she shouts back.

Jon's arm stiffens like it wants to push her off her rock, injured ankle and all. Instead, he counts to ten, grinds his teeth. The tension between them is definitely stressing out Aron. Maybe that's why he hasn't come out from behind his tree yet.

Well, okay, he'll give Aron a little break, get camp and supper going, make a splint, and persuade Korka to keep the ankle elevated. He's getting to use all the stuff he learned in the online training he did to prepare for EMT certification — even if his difficult patient is glaring at him. And even though they maybe shouldn't have started a campfire, if Aron's right that there are other people around here.

Aron, Aron. The kid never, ever gets snarky or wanders off. Not before today, anyway. It has been a few minutes too long, and Jon is worried. "Aron! Enough. Get over here!" he calls out.

No reply, no movement. Alarmed now, he leaps up and starts searching, ever more frantically.

Aron wanders well away from camp, thoughts all jumbled up in his head. The clan is besieged, ragged, and starving. But the young Viking hunter has finally found the courage to break free and set off to slay a beast in the primeval forest. Big Viking would not have let him go but for his need to apply potions to the maiden's war injuries. Soon the young hunter will return with sustenance that will revive the lost Vikings and allow them to journey forth to the legendary Great Hall, where they will recover from the heavy losses of battle, eat and drink well, and prepare for their homecoming of triumph in less than a moon.

The young hunter breathes deeply, savouring the fresh mountain air, unafraid just this once in the gathering dusk. He wills the creatures of the shadows to appear, his weapon in his hands.

A twig snaps, and he freezes. He feels the eyes of an observer upon him. His hand tightens on his slingshot, and he wonders briefly about the wisdom of his solo expedition. But his superpower of perception informs him that it is a curious human rather than a malicious beast. A human that does not know it has been sensed, and has no intention of being discovered. Fine. The young hunter judges it safest to give no indication that he is aware of the interloper's presence.

Besides, he now senses prey some paces ahead. He advances slowly on the food source, mouth salivating, as he is drawn to a shadowy bush. He's surprised to find a hare there, in a simple wire snare. Very freshly caught, as it has not yet struggled enough to suffocate itself.

His eyes scan the darkening ancient woods, and his mind does battle with itself. It is another warrior's catch, and therefore dishonourable to take. But the lifeblood of the clan depends on his success this very day. The gods of survival surely provided this opportunity. And so he leans forward, lifts the creature from the snare, and snaps its neck as quickly as he can.

Jon runs, searches, and calls for twenty minutes before sprinting back to camp to check whether Aron has shown up there. Korka has crawled from where she was sitting to the pot, which she is stirring. Both are startled by twigs cracking to their left. They turn in that direction, then glance at each other.

"Aron?" Jon calls out. No answer. Shivers travel down his spine. "Stay here," he whispers. Like Korka's going anywhere on that ankle.

The crackle is too heavy to be a bird, too light to be a bear or adult moose. Too stealthy to be —

A crashing sound comes from the opposite direction, like a sasquatch clomping through the brush.

Jon stands in commando stance with his knife pulled from its sheath, bear-spray can in his other hand, ready to defend his camp and family. He feels strong, alert, and capable, fully alive.

He's ready to plunge the knife into whatever is charging, but Aron materializes from the dusk, his face lit up. Triumphantly, he holds something up in his right hand: a freshly killed hare.

"Aron!" Jon says in relief, as his ragged little brother dances around the two of them, whooping. "You caught us some supper! But where have you been? How far did you go? You can't just disappear like that. It's not safe, and it had us —"

"Hurray, Aron!" Korka cuts Jon off with a joyful shout and a hug for her younger brother.

Jon knows the instant he starts to skin the hare that it has not died by a slingshot wound. Aron merely snapped its neck. How would he have gotten close enough to do that? Did he set their snare? Nope. It's still sitting on top of the backpack. Rob another person's snare? But there's no one around. He steals a glance at Aron, but his brother keeps his own eyes locked on his prize, a smile stretched across his dirt-caked face.

"See anyone?" Jon asks. His eyes and ears are straining for further sounds, but all is quiet.

Aron shakes his head.

Jon takes his time preparing the hare, wondering and worrying. Even as he guts the carcass, he's on full alert, ready to whip his knife out and use it on an approaching enemy. His eyes scan the forest constantly as the meat cooks on their small campfire, its juices dripping and the fragrance rising in a cloud that wafts its way to their eager nostrils.

But his mind is churning. *Where did this hare came from? If Aron didn't kill it, someone else has to be close by.*

FOURTEEN

Given Korka's injury, Jon has no choice but to declare at least a couple of weeks' rest in what Aron has named the Valley of the Hares, which the topo maps indicate is at about 1,500 metres elevation. Each day, he and Aron work hard at pursuing food for their gnawing stomachs, while their impatient sister keeps her foot raised and immobile — most of the time — and her tongue busy bemoaning the fact she can't climb trees for birds' eggs, even though it's still at least two weeks too early, or help them gather firewood.

Instead, when she thinks they're not looking, she crawls around to logs where insects have burrowed, gathering sawdust for fire tinder. Or, Jon has observed, she plucks leaves from Labrador tea shrubs and needles from blue spruce trees (which contain vitamin C) to make nutritious teas. At least this shuts her up for a while, thankfully. Sometimes she sits in the tent, leaning on one pack with her foot raised on another, and whittles Norse figures on pieces of wood for Aron, the shavings scattering across the tent floor.

Between Aron and Jon, a feisty hunting competition has developed. On the second day of their enforced waiting period, Jon snares a red squirrel. Three days later, Aron is helping him dig a toilet hole when the boy rises and places a finger over his mouth. Jon can hear nothing, but as usual, he accepts Aron's almost supernatural sense of what's going on around them. Aron looks this way and that, then seems to figure out where the noise is coming from. He beckons Jon, who follows, putting his senses of smell and hearing on full alert. Person? Animal? Danger? Food source? From Aron's relatively relaxed shoulders, he decides his brother is more curious than frightened.

When Aron stops dead at the edge of a clearing and crouches down, Jon follows suit. Is this a game? Nope. He knows Aron better than that. Even Dad would often trust Aron's hunches without argument or a shred of evidence.

"Elk," Aron whispers. Jon searches the clearing in vain until he finally spots a shadow loitering on the far end. Pleased he has binoculars at the ready, Jon focuses in to see the elegant creature, a young leggy cow, pacing nervously, huffing steam into the cool air. She's very much like a deer except for her proportionally smaller ears, more powerful body, more defined white rump, and longer neck and legs, both of which are black, in contrast to her brown body. No antlers, of course, being female — although a male has no more than bumps till April. Elk are rarely alone, he recalls. There must be more somewhere nearby in the woods.

Aron turns to Jon with a high-wattage smile, like he has managed to drag his brother to a newly released superhero movie that's about to begin. They have front-row seats, that's for sure. *All that's missing is popcorn — and a video-cam,* Jon muses. Or better yet, a rifle. He measures whether they're in any danger here at the edge of the meadow and decides it's low risk. But he confirms his knife is on his belt, just in case, and reaches out slowly to grab a large stick, then pulls a second one to his chest to hand Aron.

The elk turns this way and that, then finally breaks cover to amble into the clearing. That's when the sun catches something gold behind her, something with a black-tipped tail, crouching. The cougar stalks, slowly and gracefully, then accelerates at an astonishing speed, so powerful and efficient in its movement that it mesmerizes Jon. It licks its lips, whiskers quivering, now less than the length of a semi-trailer away from the elk. It accelerates into a blur and, in just a few impressive leaps, lands on the elk's flanks. Jon sucks in his breath and feels Aron lean into him.

The elk, caught unaware until the last second, bucks her body so high up into the air that the two are flying for a moment before they crash down, kicking, rolling, somersaulting as one. The elk's eerie vocals sound half like a horse whinny and half like a human scream. At one point, when she is standing on all four legs, the cougar springs from a prone position in front of her and sinks its teeth into her throat. She's breathing hard, her chest heaving, but doesn't whip her head about, which would end things faster. A moment later, they're both on the ground, eight legs kicking furiously, entangled in an intense wrestling match. If the elk were a bull with antlers, Jon would expect the antler tips to puncture the cougar's stomach at this stage. Instead, the head-butting is just one element in the vicious battle for life.

One gaze into the elk's large eyes, which are wild with panic, and Jon has to look away. He tries to close his ears to the sounds of distress and pain. Finally, the cougar's firm hold on her throat makes the elk go still. Knowing that, unlike wolves, who eat leisurely, cougars consume their prey quickly, Jon leaps to his feet.

"Now!" he says, not bothering to whisper, and Aron stands like he knew all along their part in this movie's climax. Emboldened by their experience with the moose, the two wave their sticks and shout like hoodlums as they approach the fallen elk.

Unsheathing his precious knife, Jon shouts aggressively at the cat, as if he were a caveman accustomed to stealing kills every day. "Get! Out of here, kitty. Scram!" The cougar merely flicks its tail. "We won't take much," he adds. "A few chunks and we're gone. Plenty left for you and your family."

The elk's killer glares and initially refuses to back away, seemingly unimpressed by such young humans attempting a heist. The cougar is way more threatening than the wolves, and Jon is having a hard time pretending he's not nervous. Eventually, though, the cougar settles defiantly not far from the motionless elk and rests its handsome head on its large paws, like a scolded but unrepentant house cat.

Good thing it's two against one, Jon reflects. A family of cats would have been an entirely different matter. He and Aron both study the rim of the clearing from one end to another. Nothing. No one. As with the moose, Jon quickly carves out some chunks of steaming meat, then backs off, never taking his eyes off the now-pacing cougar. The brothers back off and have reached tree cover when the cougar pounces on its well-earned dinner. They lose no time at all carrying their dripping prize, a week's worth of meat, back to camp.

After Jon cooks some up, he, Aron, and Korka rip into the meat like starving Neanderthals. He smokes some of the meat, then boils the bones to capture every last nutrient in a soup.

In the coming days, Aron's happiness seems to grow with every hare he delivers. As much as Jon appreciates the protein, it bothers him that Aron is growing less obedient.

"Aron, you need to stay in camp when I'm not around," he admonishes one day.

Aron merely shrugs and looks the other way.

"Wait for me if you want to leave camp to hunt hares, do you understand?"

Eyes flashing, Aron says, "I understand." But his lip is upturned and next time Jon searches for him in camp, he's nowhere to be found.

Jon continues to worry that the hares belong to someone else — someone who couldn't be far away, and who might follow Aron back to camp. He even shadows Aron several times, but somehow, Aron either manages to ditch Jon or doesn't return with a hare.

"Aron, when you leave camp, like you're not supposed to, do you ever see smoke or people?" Jon asks.

Aron shakes his head vigorously.

"I haven't seen anything either," Korka responds, perhaps relieved it's Aron getting the heat from Jon these days.

They catch a few fish in the nearby stream. But perhaps most amazingly, their young Viking finally manages to take down a ruffed grouse. Jon helps him pluck it while congratulating him again and again. Aron beams like he's won a Nordic cruise.

"Korka tried to find berries to stuff it with, but none around yet," Jon says, giving his brother a third congratulatory hug.

It's food, but still nowhere near enough, and Jon is worried about their energy sapping away. The moose pemmican is mere memory, and the elk is going fast. He should have chopped more hunks of meat off both the moose and the elk for smoking, but it seemed so much at the time, and there were the waiting predators.

Eating a diet of mostly rabbit meat can kill you, he remembers reading in a wilderness-survival book. Digesting rabbits supposedly uses up more vitamins and minerals than their meat supplies. "They eventually strip your body of essential elements," the book informed him.

And weasels aren't worth the effort: too little meat. It's lucky they're getting other meats and fish occasionally.

For the weeks it takes Korka's ankle to heal, their catches are enough for Jon to maintain his goal of keeping them here in the woods, surviving by their wits and determination. They still have their most important items: water-purification tablets, waterproof matches, tent, topographical map, compass, folding saw, headlamps, and the one-burner stove with fuel, which they conserve for rainy days or times they fear that someone might see their fire smoke. But what really keeps them going are visions of reaching the mining town. The low valley must be green by now, and they are eager to reach it — fantasy picket fence, wind-stirred lace curtains, and all.

They've been in the camp for what Jon guesses is three or four weeks — and Korka's ankle is pretty much mended — when he first notices things going missing. A pack of waterproof matches. Must have been misplaced. A rain poncho. That's more baffling. Then their folding saw.

Jon is panicking, furious. "Aron, did you borrow the saw?" he shouts. "And have you lost a rain poncho somewhere?"

Despite Aron's valuable contributions of hares, it bothers Jon a lot that his brother keeps heading out on his own, sometimes not returning for an hour or two. It's a development he doesn't like one bit, but laying down rules does no good anymore. Aron just defies them.

Aron shakes his head vigorously.

"And I know we had two more packs of matches. Korka? Aron? Have you gone through a whole box this week?"

"Stop accusing us!" Korka stops whittling shapes into a walking stick Aron has brought her.

"But the saw!" Jon erupts. "Someone has lost it! We can't survive without it. And someone must have borrowed the rain poncho from my pack since last night."

"Ravens?" Korka suggests in a voice that's tense but attempting to sound bored. "Maybe they build nests using saws, matchsticks, and ponchos now?"

"Guys," Jon says in a calmer but firm tone, "things are going missing. What's going on?"

From the corner of his eye, he catches Aron squirming a little. Like he knows more than he's saying. Jon decides to keep his mouth shut and eyes wide open.

That night, as they crawl into their sleeping bags, he pushes his backpack into the protected entryway between the zipping door and flaps as usual, but he doesn't zip the door down all the way. Positioning his head and one arm partway into the space, he ties one of the pack's straps around his wrist and closes his eyes, willing himself to stay awake all night.

Well past midnight, he wakes when the bag moves a millimetre or two, just enough to alert him. He holds his breath and squeezes his eyes shut. The thief unzips the bag without a sound and reaches deep into it to remove something.

The hint of a jingle identifies their can of cash! Hardly has the arm withdrawn than he leaps up, pulls the strap from his wrist, shoves his feet into his boots, and is outside. A shadowy figure sprints away, and he gives chase in the slushy snow, shouting.

Under the sliver of a moon, he can see the thief is dressed in dark clothes, complete with hiking boots, and is swift on his feet. How the silhouette can dart so fast through the forest with no headlamp, Jon has no clue, but when he switches his own on and trains it on the burglar, the mysterious stranger doubles his speed, twisting and turning around tree trunks.

The shadow takes a flying leap over a stream, catching Jon by surprise. Despite his quick reactions, Jon ends up with one boot stuck between two fallen branches on the far side.

"Why?" he shouts. "Why steal from campers who have so little? We're kids! We'll starve without that money!"

To his surprise, the figure halts and whirls around. "He keeps stealing my hares. This is payback. Fair's fair."

"Who? What?" Jon, astonished, barely registers that the voice is a girl's, not a man's. "You mean my brother has been stealing hares from you? I'll pay you for them if you want, but don't steal our gear and all our money, please. We're hungry, and we're —"

"— in hiding," she says, stepping closer, but not close enough for Jon to lunge at her. She's in a black down parka, black jeans, and a red-and-black-checkered hunter's cap with oversized earflaps. "Three of you. A sulky girl with an injury, a boy who almost never talks, and one who's way too bossy."

Jon squints into the dark and frees his boot. "And you are …?"

"None of your business."

At that, she bounds away with a crackle of twigs and all but disappears into the darkness. He leaps up and goes after her full speed, adrenalin fuelling his determination. They race over the uneven ground for what seems like ages, until he manages to catch up and tackle her. The money can falls to the ground.

"Keep some of the money if you want, even the poncho, but give us back our saw!"

"Ouch. Get off me!"

Her arms are flailing, and she manages to thrust an elbow into his jaw. The flash of pain unleashes anger. He pins her down so she can't move at all, even puts his hand over her mouth. A pitiful attempt at a scream escapes her, and her bulging eyes, illuminated by his headlamp, make him loosen his hold a little.

"I'm not going to hurt you. Just stop fighting for a minute. Are you alone?"

"None of your business."

He guesses she is. "Look, you don't have to tell me your story, but I'll tell you ours. Ravens got some of our food, then my brother was sick, and then my sister sprained her ankle. So, we're barely surviving right now."

"Uh-huh," she says, going calm.

He releases her arms. She stares at the can beside them, then pushes it reluctantly at him. With deep relief he grabs it, fishes out some crinkled five-dollar bills, and places them in her hands. "For the hares. How about the other stuff?"

She shrugs. Then her body relaxes slightly, and her dark eyes widen. "Are you the kids whose parents were killed in an avalanche more than two months ago?"

His jaw loosens and his chest tightens. "Maybe." So she has seen a newspaper lately; either she hasn't been here long, or she's visited a town for supplies at some point.

"When my sister's ankle is mended enough, we're moving on," he says. "We'll use this money to get stuff from Wolfsburg. I don't need to tell anyone you exist. I couldn't care less what you're up to. You can have the poncho and matches, as long as you return the saw — and leave us alone."

She removes the fur-lined hunter's cap and shakes her head. Her long red hair spills down over her shoulders and her moonlit freckles are now visible on her face. She's close to Jon's age, maybe a little older. Why is she hanging out here in the wilderness? *Gutsy* is a word that inserts itself into Jon's brain, followed by *pretty*. *Forget it, Jon, you idiot.*

Her silence bugs him. "You talk about as much as my little brother," he dares to say.

That produces a faint smile.

"Anyone else been around here? Hunters or searchers or whatever?"

She shakes her head.

"Why'd you let my brother steal your hares?" Jon asks, hardly believing he's having a sort-of conversation with someone besides his siblings for the first time in weeks. He had no idea how much he missed talking with other human beings.

"Just curious," she says. "I like spying on the three of you. Can't believe you snared a red squirrel and chased a cougar off an elk carcass."

"Next time I'll share our meat, if we get lucky again."

Why was he blurting this out? Especially to a thief and possible fellow runaway who might have her own posse after her in these woods. "How long have you been —?"

"None of your —"

"Okay, I get it." He grabs her hat. "I'll return this when you return the saw."

"I'll return the saw tomorrow." She glowers and grabs the hat back. He lets her, for no good reason. "Bon voyage and good riddance," she says.

Then she leaps up and is gone like a phantom in the darkness.

FIFTEEN

Jon gets up and stares after her, feeling suddenly cold and lonely. He looks into the dark, thawing woods around him and realizes he has no idea how to get back to the stream where his boot got momentarily stuck, or to camp. What kind of leader abandons his charges and gets lost in the middle of the night? He was protecting their property, sure, but their lives are more important.

A terrifying thought occurs to him: What if the girl has some kind of accomplice who circled around to their camp while he was with her?

Sweat runs down his forehead even in the cold. His heart races, and his knees feel weak. Rubbing his jaw

where the girl punched him, he walks slowly in a direction that feels right — that he desperately hopes is right,
anyway.

He knows he's even more lost when a hoot sounds
overhead. Uh-oh, he has gone deeper into the forest.
Looking up, he sees an owl. Clearly, the owl sees him, too
— probably sees him as a fool. Owls, he recalls, have the
best night vision in the animal or bird kingdom. Night
vision is what he could use now. Night vision is something hunters use occasionally, too, he remembers with a
tightening chest. It's a fear he hasn't voiced to his siblings,
but the wilderness around them is rich in the wildlife
that hunters covet: mountain goats, bighorn sheep, elk,
deer, moose, caribou, wolves, coyotes, wolverine, cougar,
lynx, and bears. Some of these are more active at night,
and less on edge. It's a perfect time for people with guns
and night-vision equipment or thermal scopes to move
about, legally or illegally, in season or not. But why is he
thinking about this now? Because an owl hooted?

He freezes and listens carefully to see if something
else started this train of thought in his mind. Standing
stock-still in a forest at night hoping for silence is idiot-
ic, of course. Things rustle in the underbrush close by,
trees creak, owls hoot, and far away, wolves howl. Even
the most unimaginative visitor can conjure up something
frightening. Especially when there's a crunch of footsteps.
Wait! Footsteps?

Yes, and men's hushed voices — the most terrifying
sound of all. He swears he is hearing voices both a good
distance away and too nearby. People moving stealthily.

Maybe with hunting rifles pointed at him, waiting for him to appear in their night-vision scopes. Has he lost his mind or are his ears truly picking up a hunting party? It's not hunting season, but poachers can get away with murder in these parts. The owl hoots again and flaps away. He makes like a statue and counts to twenty to calm himself.

The first gunshot fells him flat to the ground. *Please, please, be shooting at deer, not at me, my family, or the girl thief.*

The second gunshot almost makes him soil his pants. He shivers with fear, clutching himself, oblivious to the cold creeping into his bones.

Shouts definitely not imagined are far away, but carry well in the night. They're joyous cries, like hunters make when they've achieved a kill. If he stays flat on the ground, unmoving, hypothermia will wrap him in her icy arms, but that's better than a scope picking him out and mistaking him for a trophy. Or discovering he's a human, and withholding fire to radio him in. Are these hunters connected with the girl? He thinks not. He imagines her hiding somewhere, shaking in her boots, equally terrified.

Eventually, the voices retreat, farther and farther away until he can hear absolutely nothing now except the rustlings of normal nightlife. Not even an overhead owl pitying him for being lost in dangerous terrain. It's time to move.

Thorny branches scratch his face, and roots trip him, but he carries on, limbs aching and a heaviness growing in his chest. Getting back to the tent is the most important thing in his life right now. His parents would be quick to call him out on his error in judgment, leaving his siblings alone. It's almost as dumb a mistake as the snow-cave thing.

Just hours earlier he'd imagined his own brother and sister as a weighty pack and fantasized about having a break from them. What a jerk. He must never leave them alone again, not for any reason. At least not until they get to the mining town. They're just kids, with no idea how to survive without him. What if they heard the gunshots? Though he suspects they're too far away. What if they wake up now and panic when they discover he isn't there? They might venture out into the inky dark looking for him, and run into —

Jon's nostrils prickle at a foul smell. He freezes as he hears an ominous huffing ahead, followed by something crashing through the vegetation. He halts and reaches to his belt for bear spray and his knife. Too late, he realizes he left them behind in the tent. He's defenceless and lost, and has survived the night hunters only to be attacked by a —

Instinctively, he leaps to the nearest tree, shimmying up its branches. A giant, dark figure lumbers into sight and stops in the snow beneath Jon's perch, then raises a hairy arm toward him while emitting a bellowing growl. Jon's entire body vibrates like a sapling in a windstorm. But there shouldn't be any bears out of hibernation for another week or two! And bears usually sleep till almost dawn. *Just my luck to encounter an early riser, in both senses*, Jon thinks in shock.

The slice of moon peeks out from behind a cloud as if startled out of hiding itself. In that microsecond, Jon sees coarse yellow fur, flashing eyes, and huge claws. Nearly losing his grip, he thanks fate it's a grizzly, not a black bear. Grizzlies don't climb trees.

The giant doesn't stick around for long, but Jon knows better than to climb down and risk another encounter, or to try and find the campsite in the pitch black. Better to stay alive and rescue his siblings in the morning than to thrash through the deep brush trying to find them, only to get mauled.

He sizes up the situation. With her injured ankle, Korka won't come looking for him, and Aron, if frightened, will stick close to his sister. Jon's throat is parched, and he shivers. Guilt descends.

Tucked into a crook where branch meets trunk, he places the tin of money in his lap and feels a humiliating sense of failure envelop him. He has brought his brother and sister deep into the wilderness, only to commit one disastrous mistake after another. The ravens, the blister, Aron's fever, Korka's ankle, the suspicious hares, and now getting lost within hearing distance of night hunters. *Mom, Dad, I'm a lousy substitute for you.*

He lowers his head to his hands — filthy, gashed-up hands — and heaves a sob. Then it's like a geyser dislodges its plug and all hell breaks loose. Shaking, blubbering, dissolving into a fountain of tears, he groans and slobbers, streams of snot pouring from his nostrils. He wraps his arms around himself and plays everything back: Aron clutching his father's ankles to keep him from leaving, then thumping his mother to stop her. His father stepping off the cornice; his mother rushing out the door and then risking her own life to save her husband's. The second avalanche burying her alive. Jon sways back and forth, in danger of falling out of the tree but not caring. He relives himself chasing after Aron, hoping against hope he might help save Mom, performing CPR on her, then hauling his siblings back into the house, all three of them stricken. The Vines, the social worker, the reporters, the gut-wrenching visit to the morgue that he wishes with all his being he could erase from his memory, and the dismal, cheapskate memorial service.

Sorry for your loss, sorry for your loss, sorry for your loss.

He trembles and teeters. His eyes leak and his nose runs, and he moans in tune with the wind. He misses his parents so much, yet has hardly had time to think about them. Now grief has hit him like a spray of bullets. He can no longer dodge, hide, or fight the agony, even if it seriously depletes the energy he needs to survive. He has locked it away for too long, too deep inside.

Shaking and shivering and clinging to his precarious perch, he finally lapses into a semi-conscious state. He dreams that slabs of snow let loose from the sloped valley all around their current location. The frozen fragments tumble and spill toward his siblings' tent from every side, isolating him in his tree. Frozen white limbs of avalanche victims stick out of the snow like gruesome twigs. As the avalanches reach the campsite, they halt just short of the little green tent, piling up until it's surrounded by high, white walls Jon can't get a grip on, can't clamber up over, can't dig through. He hears Korka and Aron scream and scream, unheard by any other human being, as they wait to die by freezing and starvation. He brought them here so they could stay together, remain a family. But now there's no one to save the two of them. He's helpless and fated to die himself. There's no one to reverse his reckless, arrogant plan to smuggle his siblings into the unforgiving wilderness of these mountains.

As dawn breaks, he rubs his crusted eyelids and rouses himself. Though exhausted and drained of all feeling, he clutches the tin of money and issues himself an order: Think only of your immediate situation and the days ahead. They must break camp today so they can reach the mining town before they weaken any further, or implode, or meet the hunters.

SIXTEEN

On the morrow, the maiden arrives for Aron earlier than usual, when the sky is still a deep violet, before the chickadees and nuthatches break into morning song. Aron doesn't hear her, just knows she's lingering, waiting in their usual clearing, now plagued with mud from the melting snow. He doesn't question the unusually primitive hour when he opens his eyes and looks about the tent.

He observes Jon's empty sleeping bag tossed in one corner, as if he rose lacking in dignity and time. Jon's backpack is half-open and tipped over in the entryway, his boots gone. He's probably out gathering firewood in his true and steady fashion. It will be good for cooking whatever victuals Aron returns with.

Korka opens one eye as he rises and dons his tunic and breeches. "Where's Jon?" she mumbles.

Aron mimes wood-chopping, so his sister's eyes roll closed again, and soon she returns to heavy breathing. Aron steps outside, fills both his and Korka's water bottles with filtered ice-cold creek water, and reaches back into the abode to place hers neatly by her side. His eyes rest on her raised ankle. Then he squeezes them shut and tries to send healing powers her way, like he does every day, even if it might be silly. Finally, he hurries to the clearing, his slingshot sticking out of his back pocket.

There she is, leaning casually against a tree in her patched jacket, torn black jeans, worn hiking boots, and hunter's cap. She greets him with a warm smile, like always, a smile he is certain resembles that of Freya, the most powerful Nordic goddess. She has her slingshot in hand already, and she nods to their target for the morning: marks she has made on a tree. He loves how she understands the beauty of communicating without talking.

"Did you hear anything unusual last night?" she asks.

He shakes his head and searches her face to assess whether he should be worried.

"There were hunters, but they're long gone now, no danger to us," she says.

He nods, certain she used her powers to make them disappear.

A red squirrel chitters at them from high above as she hits the first tree marking, bull's eye, like she always does. He raises his slingshot and takes his time, needing to impress her, to prove that her coaching is having an effect on her vassal's skills.

The young hunter hits within a finger's width of the tree's mark, and this satyr with the brilliant red hair rewards him with a gentle hand pressed to the top of his head, just like his mother used to do. He leans into the touch, never wanting the warm hand to stray. Mayhap she is his mother, chosen to return as this slender, quiet, nameless maiden. Or she could be a Norse deity come down to comfort and help him, but that would not explain the Celtic cross around her neck or the freckles on her face.

In truth, from the moment they met, he knew she was human, and a girl without adults in her life. Like him and his siblings.

He also senses she's a girl with a troubled soul. Her body emanates hurt and loneliness like the orange flare around the black rim of a solar eclipse, though she has no way of knowing he can read that. These make her both kind and potentially volatile. Kind for now.

What's important is that his brother and sister know nothing of this girl-woman, nor the slingshot lessons. It's his secret to keep. When she touches his arm, he understands not to aim at the tree on the next round as planned. Instead, he follows her eyes to a hare in a meadow beyond, a creature lit by a morning sunray. His teacher nods encouragement. He loads a smooth stone and takes his time, craving beyond any need in the universe to prove himself to his mentor this morning, to kill his first hare by slingshot.

The sharp stone finds its mark, true and steady. But some uncanny instinct makes him reload faster than he has ever fitted rounded stones to rubber tubing. Without questioning why, he raises his eyes higher on the lightening horizon. Though it's not yet visible, he feels a tiny object speeding toward them, buzzing very softly like a hummingbird. Body tensed, he lets his rock loose even before the object appears, then catches the girl staring at him open-mouthed. His shot brings down the drone before its camera lens turns toward them. As one, then, he and his mentor stumble backward, swing around, and race for Aron's campsite, their boots pounding the hard ground.

Korka wakes up late, troubled by dreams of her parents lying in coffins, hammering on the lids from inside to get out. No one hears their screams but her, and she's far away in the woods with a sprained ankle. She wakes gasping and sweaty, her face wet with tears. *We didn't even put them in coffins. We let their ashes float on a breeze over the mountain. Yet they're with us, somehow. Aren't you, Mom and Dad?*

She sits up and takes stock of the overbright tent walls. She has overslept, but her siblings seem to have let her do that. Such a rare burst of thoughtfulness.

She rolls over onto a full water bottle and vaguely recalls Aron leaving to chop wood with Jon, or something like that. It was nice of Aron to refill her bottle before he left. She lets the thought chase away the remains of her troubling nightmare.

"Jon? Aron?" she calls out.

No reply. Good, they've finally recognized that she has recovered enough to look after herself. About time they stopped treating her like an invalid. And Jon must have undergone some kind of miraculous conversion to finally understand that Aron can help him gather firewood (duh), and that she needs a break from babysitting him.

She sits up straight-backed in her sleeping bag, leg still raised on a pack, letting the luxury of the thought wash over her in the light made green by the tent walls. She senses a sunny, crisp morning. Wonderful, quiet aloneness for the first time in weeks.

Better yet, the formerly swollen, black-and-blue ankle that was all Jon's fault is mostly back to normal. She feels like she can move around more today, help with chores, maybe even break camp and get out of here. The delay has totally sucked. It has been tough living on a few scraggly hares and the food pack's fast-disappearing freeze-dried soups. It's never enough. She's so hungry. They need real food. A deer or something. She presses her fingers into her ribs, more prominent than they were just weeks before.

What did Jon say? A couple of days to get to the mining village? That's where they'll have a house and plant a garden and be able to shop at the general store nearby. When the weather warms, she can make blueberry muffins from the wild blueberries on the bushes outside their door. There will be old musty books on the bookshelves, wooden deck chairs on the porch, and a stray cat that will cuddle up to her. She pictures a barbecue for grilling steaks in the backyard, a panorama of white-capped mountains surrounding them, fawns peering in the window, and maybe best of all, a river just behind the cabin to bathe in.

She feels unbelievably grimy right now, like dirt has burrowed into every pore in her body. It may not bother Jon and Aron, but she's dying to get clean for the first time in a long time. An ice-water dip would be just the thing. And afterward, catching a rainbow trout or two.

She wriggles into her worn, holey jeans and sweatshirt, hobbles out of the tent, and looks around. No boys! Just her and a fine day. She limps through what's left of the wet snow to the creek, dips in their cooking pot, and feels excitement building. She'll prove to the guys that she's all well again and able to prepare their breakfast. She breaks bits of birch bark off nearby trees, knowing it has good resin for getting a campfire blazing. She lights the fire by applying sparks from their flint and steel to dry tinder, annoyed that Jon and Aron have lost the last of the matches but proud of her own skills at nursing a flame from wood shavings. She eases the food bag down from its rope and locates the oatmeal. Not much left, but surely they're almost within reach of that general store now. They can buy food and fuel there, as well as a new folding saw.

She wonders how Jon managed to lose theirs. At least they have the map and compass. *But if I were leading*, she thinks, *they would never have disappeared. And we never would have had to travel down that scree slope. We'd be way farther along.*

As Jon spots camp from a viewpoint that morning, he identifies Korka eating from a pot. Relieved, he starts downhill. He's just about to call out to Korka when he hears something, or someone, galloping toward the camp from the other direction. A charging moose? A hunter? He halts in disbelief when he spots Aron, expression wild and sweat shining on his forehead, with a tall adult in pursuit. The girl from last night!

As Jon sprints toward them, he sees Korka limp to a tree beside the tent. Aron whizzes by her, then Korka trips the pursuer and applies her best move, an open-hand strike on the girl's neck with the heel of her right hand. *Whoomph.* Jon imagines air leaving the girl's lungs as her body hits the muddy ground, her eyes wide.

"Guys, I'm coming!" he shouts.

But Aron reaches his sister first. "No, Korka!" he shouts. "Leave her alone! Pack up. We have to hide, fast!"

Jon and the girl on the ground lock eyes. "You again?" Jon says.

"Huh?" Korka is saying.

In the daylight, he can see that the redhead's freckled face is deeply grimed and tanned, and her bright hair tangled. It confirms Jon's theory that she's been living rough for a while. A slingshot and the hunter's cap are shoved into her jeans pockets. She looks strong and proud as she leaps up, glares at Korka, and joins Aron in dismantling their tent hyperfast.

"Help, Jon!"

How does she know his name? Korka is staring at him like he's a traitor.

"Follow us, Korka," the girl orders. "Your ankle's healed enough to keep up. Now!" she adds darkly, tossing Korka a heavy pack. "Before Search and Rescue catches up with us."

Jon and Korka might not know what's going on, but one look at Aron's nod and they shoulder their packs, grab the tent bag, and start to splash across the stream.

The tall girl is hauling the food bag. She'd better not be stealing it. Jon glances behind them and sees they've managed to leave nothing at all but footprints and a cold firepit. If Search and Rescue is really on their tail — and Aron wouldn't be following this girl if they weren't — they'll have no concrete proof of who camped there, unless they have sniffer dogs.

Minutes later, the girl they're following blindly slows. "SAR is after us," she says, stuffing her hair into her ugly hunter's cap. "I'll show you where to hide."

Jon scans the forest behind them. Shaking his head, he steps up his pace and follows, grabbing the food bag off the girl. Korka looks utterly confused but seems to know this isn't the time to ask what's happening.

The forest girl is fast, that's for sure, and seems to know her way around these dense woods. Within twenty minutes, and despite Korka's ankle slowing them down, the girl stops abruptly and points down at the snow-covered forest floor.

Huh? All three stare at the strange girl.

She leans down and lifts a rock. The forest floor seems to rise with it — one square metre of it, anyway. It turns out to be a lid, a square of woven branches disguised by snow, dirt, rocks, and vegetation. The entry reveals dirt-hacked steps leading to a small underground space.

"A bunker," Jon declares. His voice fails to hide the fact that he's impressed. "But Aron is severely claustrophobic. He can't handle this small space."

"He'll go in if he has to," the girl says in a no-nonsense voice, turning to Aron like it's an order rather than an observation.

"No, he won't." And then it dawns on Jon. "You're Leah, aren't you?" he says accusingly. "Leah Green, the runaway from Rockvale."

The girl narrows her eyes, her face pinched. "Get in," she says. "I'm trying to help you."

"Are you? Your parents tried to hire us to find you. Looks like I've succeeded." And how do they know the bunker isn't a trap?

Men's voices sound from well behind. As Jon and Leah stand locked in some kind of standoff, Aron lowers himself into the hole, tugging Korka with him. The two settle into the tiny cellar with their backs to the frozen earth wall. Leah nods her approval, then throws all their gear down to one side of them. She even removes her home-made wooden slingshot from her jeans pocket and tosses it on top. Turning to glower at Jon, she continues to hold up one corner of the lid.

Seeing Aron's thumbs-up, Jon makes up his mind and quickly climbs in. As the heavy lid closes over their heads, he drops into a cross-legged position between his siblings and puts his arms around them. He draws them into a tight hug, smelling dirt and sweat and home. He can feel Aron shuddering. Yet the boy manages not to scream out or try to break away.

He hears what must be the girl sweeping the snow above them with something. A twig broom? If Leah is a runaway, too, why isn't she hiding with them? Why did she toss in her slingshot? And if she's ditching them, can they lift the door to escape, or will they be trapped in this dark hole, the chill slowly robbing them of life?

SEVENTEEN

In the pitch black of the bunker, Jon feels Korka reach for Aron's hands. "Shhh, shhh," she says. His moans and wriggling stop. Even in the dark, Jon feels Aron summon the courage to sit quiet and still.

"Who *is* that girl?" Korka whispers to Jon.

"Her name's Leah Green. She's a runaway. Her parents wanted to hire Mom and Dad to find her."

A stampede of boots invades a space somewhere above. The vibrations send snow sliding down into their hole, and Jon fears the branches above may not hold if anyone steps on the disguised lid.

He feels Korka stroke Aron's hair and is amazed at his brother's bravery.

Then he hears a voice he recognizes. "Are you the moron who downed a law-enforcement drone with a rock?" demands Officer Vine, huffing.

So, it seems Officer Vine is with the SAR detachment, and has finally caught up to them after all these weeks. But a drone? Near here? Jon's mind races. Who was it searching for? Did Leah actually take it down? Is that what brought them storming here, and is that why Leah tossed her slingshot into the pit with them? *She was spying on us for a week, armed all the time. What kind of protector does that make me?*

He pictures Officer Vine standing there with his chest puffed out, a finger touching the handcuffs he'd love to clamp on someone and a posse of SAR people behind him, all giving Leah a scowling once-over. She's clearly a teenager in the wilderness, which will make them suspicious, but since she's from a different area and was never officially reported missing, Officer Vine is unlikely to know her name or face.

"I haven't seen a drone and wouldn't know how to take one down if I had." Leah's voice is firm and fearless. "I'm here on my own."

Jon pictures her poised, with arms crossed and hunter's cap pulled low over her brow, her hair tucked up inside — nobody's prisoner.

"Hmmph." The deep-voiced, suspicious response. "We'll need to take a look around your camp."

"Help yourself," she says, sounding convincingly co-operative.

There's shuffling, the sound of a pack's contents being spilled onto the ground, more cascades of snow spilling on their heads from the ground's vibrations. *Don't cough, anyone.*

"We're also looking for three kids, eleven to seventeen," Officer Vine says moments later. "They're runaways from Peakton, hiding from police. If you've seen them but didn't report them, that makes you an accomplice. There's also a reward for turning them in."

"Haven't seen anyone," she says evenly.

Whoa, how much are we worth? Jon wonders, biting his tongue at this unwelcome news.

"Yeah?" Officer Vine sounds dubious. "And what's a girl like yourself doing all alone in the middle of nowhere? Not very safe, you know."

Good thing her parents never reported her to the police, Jon reflects. So, Leah obviously dug out this dank cellar before freeze-up, which means she was out here months before her parents even contacted his. Strange.

"I can look after myself." The co-operative tone is gone.

"What's your name?" the icy voice continues.

There's silence. "I'm eighteen, as you can see." She must have whipped out a driver's licence. "Just enjoying the peace and quiet nature has to offer."

The last bit drips with sarcasm, which Jon figures isn't going to go over well with her interrogator. So, she's eighteen, which means Officer Vine can't do anything to her. But why is she protecting them? And when and how did Aron meet Leah?

By facing up to Officer Vine, she's serving as a decoy for them, he realizes. The men won't search as thoroughly as they might have otherwise. He owes her big time for this, especially now that there's a price on their heads. And that doesn't make him happy at all.

"Careful of your attitude, young lady. We're here enforcing the law. It's usually best to show respect to police officers and Search and Rescue members."

"Sorry," she says wisely — perhaps through her teeth, Jon thinks with a smile. "Leave me a card in case I see these kids," she tells the group.

These *kids*? Jon bristles. He pictures Officer Vine handing her a card, looking her up and down again, and finally signalling his posse to move on.

"Take care, Leah Green of Rockvale," Officer Vine says, enunciating the last bit slowly and purposefully.

"Good luck with your search," she replies with forced cheerfulness.

Jon, Korka, and Aron wait a long time for the bunker lid to lift. But once the men march off and the camp goes quiet, they begin to whisper. Jon finally gets the story from Aron: how he first met Leah while filching her hares, then started meeting her secretly for slingshot lessons.

"You had secret meetings with a total stranger?" Jon protests, feeling only a shrug from his brother in response.

"That's stupid and dangerous," Korka rules. So, clearly Korka never knew.

And your fault, Korka, since you obviously weren't looking after him, Jon wants to add, but doesn't.

Still, he can't help smiling when Aron describes taking down the SAR drone and Korka recounts knocking Leah down with a Krav Maga move.

"But I think my ankle has swollen up again from getting to this place," she finishes.

"That's not good." Jon hopes she's exaggerating. He doesn't tell them about chasing Leah and encountering a bear the night before, but explains how, just before the three of them left Peakton, their parents were offered money to search for Leah. "Mom asked me to help, but then ... the avalanche happened."

That brings on silence for a moment. The dark feels clingy, and their body sweat radiates an overpowering smell. It's countered by another, more welcome scent seeping through the edge of the lid: of meat stew somewhere above.

"But she's eighteen," Korka says.

"Yes, you heard how Officer Vine couldn't do much once Leah proved her age."

"Like you in a few weeks," Korka says with satisfaction.

"Shhh. She's coming," Aron whispers. A moment later, the lid lifts and daylight blinds them.

"Sorry to leave you here so long, but I wanted to be triple sure they weren't coming back. And I've made us supper. Hare stew, thanks to Aron," she says.

They stumble up the steps to a feast catered by someone with all the spices and know-how to present a gourmet hare dish.

"Wow, can you teach me how to cook like this?" Korka asks as they all tuck into the surprise dinner. Jon frowns to see his sister looking up at Leah with bright eyes. Korka only just met her! "And teach me how to snare?"

"Korka, that's *my* job," he says, "and I need you to look after —"

"Sure. Why not?" Leah says cheerfully. "If I can do it, you can."

She talks to Korka as if she's eighteen rather than fourteen, and as if the three are not leaving soon. Jon keeps his mouth zipped for now. He just watches with increasing concern the way Aron and Korka gravitate to this complete stranger, like she's some kind of celebrity, not an armed thief.

"Thanks, Leah, for dinner," he finally says, rising, "and Aron, for the hare. But it's time to gather our stuff and move on, especially now that Search and Rescue is in the area." *And now that Leah knows who we are and could change her mind about turning us in.*

"No," says Korka, head raised in defiance. "I told you I hurt my ankle again. So, now I need another rest day. Oh, and sorry, Leah, for hurting you like that."

"You just winded me," Leah says, a hand on Korka's shoulder. "You were impressive. Might get some lessons from you, if you're willing."

"Sure!" Korka radiates enthusiasm.

"Actually, Jon," Leah says, turning to him, "you're probably safer here than anywhere else right now, with them having already ruled out my campsite, and with the bunker close by if they change their minds and come back. Not to mention their drone being out of commission for the moment, thanks to Aron." She pats Aron on the head.

Jon is taken aback at the way Aron leans into that hand like … like he's known her for a long time. Like his psychic people-sussing meter isn't giving him any warnings. Like, like … like he used to do with Mom.

"We go," Jon orders, pointing a finger first at Korka, then at Aron.

"We stay," Aron says, helping himself to more hare stew and wild rice.

"*You* go," Korka says, pouty lip stuck out.

"Want me to look at your ankle?" Leah asks Korka, like there's no family crisis happening.

"Yes, please."

"No!" Jon barks. "I'm the first-aid person, and she's my sister. And we're leaving —"

"— tomorrow?" Leah suggests, rising smoothly and carrying the dishes to the creek, a satisfied smile on her lips.

EIGHTEEN

They end up staying way longer than a day. Jon is exhausted, and Leah is so generous with her food that he decides they don't need to rush to Wolfsburg for supplies yet. It's also true that Search and Rescue is less likely to return to this spot.

Despite some discomfort with being part of a foursome, and despite Korka's not watching over Aron like she should, Jon keeps delaying pulling up stakes. Even though he knows Korka's ankle is close to healed. And even though Leah has returned the folding saw and poncho. Each day, he reasons that one more day won't hurt them. He refuses to contemplate whether it has to do with his liking Leah around, too.

He watches Leah give his sister's ankle a gentle massage with special lotions every day and rebraid her hair each morning like Mom used to do, sometimes tucking the first of the season's wildflowers into it — flowers blooming because the weather has finally turned warmer.

Korka also seems over-the-top happy because Leah is totally into anything she tells her about Krav Maga. One day while the two girls are washing their clothes together in a stream, he sees Leah gift his sister with a crocheted cord necklace holding a rock, all silver and sparkly. "Iron pyrite, for protection and healing," she explains.

"Wow, thanks," Korka says.

Crazy, Jon thinks.

"It's so nice to have a girl to talk to," Jon overhears Leah confide to his sister toward the end of the week, "especially a strong, smart, brave one."

He grits his teeth and wonders why he doesn't declare that it's time to go. Then again, why would the mining town be any better? They might as well hang out here, at least for now, even if Jon can't help being annoyed that Leah increasingly overrules him on stuff.

"Korka shouldn't be getting water or doing dishes. Let her rest," Leah says. "Those are my jobs while you're my guests. I insist."

"As long as she keeps a close eye on Aron," Jon replies sternly. Korka frowns and Jon catches Leah winking at her.

Leah is suspiciously generous with her obviously limited supplies, but Jon chooses to believe she's just plain kind.

His mouth waters when she serves up hummus or tomato and cashew sauce or pad thai, all homemade dishes she dehydrated before her trip. A backcountry gourmet! She tells them she loaded up on supplies on a trip to Wolfsburg before she met them, and he gives her some cash. Later, she admits she also raided a hunter's cache she stumbled across.

To Jon's amazement, Aron has finally mastered slingshot hunting, and Korka, under Leah's tutelage, is foraging for forest edibles like some kind of expert. It means they all enjoy the occasional treat of fried, salted dandelion greens and stinging-nettle soup. Plus early-season eggs from the robins' nests that Korka is having more luck raiding. Even Jon's snare-setting has improved with a bait suggestion from their campmate: "Use this spray bottle of apple cider to coat your snare."

He can't help staring at Leah as she sprays it like she's been baiting snares all her life. Or as she sits on a boulder in a patch of spring sunlight each morning, combing out her waist-length hair, her freckled face turned to the yellow orb like she's a sun-worshipping nymph.

There's something else holding him back from moving on, too, something about the way Leah turns sparkling eyes on him when no one else is around, or the way she lets her arm brush against his when they're preparing food together. *No, Jon, don't get ideas.*

They settle into a routine of sleeping, eating, hunting, gathering, and storytelling around the campfire. Though the camaraderie and more plentiful food sources around them tempt them to relax, Jon constantly reminds them not to lower their guard. Good thing, too.

One day while he's out walking, Jon's heart picks up at the sound of voices on a far ridge. He dives into the undergrowth and holds perfectly still, eventually peering out to see four men taking turns scouring the region with binoculars. SAR, he's sure. Still looking for the lost siblings, Officer Vine no doubt having insisted they not give up.

One man points at the curl of smoke from Leah's campfire well behind Jon, and another shrugs and turns to explain. Though he can't hear the words, Jon figures the searcher is explaining about the lone teen girl hanging out there, and assuring the group that the campsite has been checked out already. They eventually turn, climb over the hill, and disappear from view.

Good riddance, Jon thinks, letting his breath out in a foggy puff. It reinforces his decision to stay a while longer, while also reminding him that the family remains on the searchers' agenda.

As Jon is stoking the fire one morning, Leah asks Korka, "Want a girls-only hike to a secret hot spring near here? We can have a really nice wash and soak."

Korka grins and hugs herself.

"Not a good idea," Jon objects. "Not safe in case anyone is around. And I'm too busy laying snares to look after Aron."

"Aron doesn't need looking after twenty-four seven. We'll be gone maybe fifteen minutes. It'll be fine," Leah says breezily.

Jon notes Korka glancing at Aron, who's busy using his slingshot to ping pebbles against a tree.

"Don't worry about him," Leah continues. "He won't move from there for hours, till he has fifty bull's eyes in a row. He's got a talent with that thing, you know. He's gotten almost as good as me now."

Fifteen minutes isn't very long, Jon reasons, and Leah and Korka aren't going to listen to him, anyway. "Aron," he says, "promise to stay here till the girls get back?"

Aron offers a thumbs-up.

Feeling uncertain, Jon gathers the snares, heads into the woods, and is almost out of earshot when he hears Korka tell Leah, "Sooo nice to get breaks from babysitting Aron."

He freezes, frowns, and positions himself behind a thick tree.

"Yeah? Why doesn't Jon take turns looking after him?"

"Aron likes me more," Korka boasts.

"Because you're not as bossy," Leah suggests, making Jon grind his teeth. "Jon kind of tells you all what to do and treats you like little kids, doesn't he?"

"Got that right!"

"I'll bet he's such a bossy pants that he doesn't even have a girlfriend?"

Korka guffaws, Leah following suit like they're co-conspirators. Not to mention that Jon can hear all this and the girls obviously don't care. Jon feels his face go hot.

"That's pretty much it," Korka says. "They dump him as soon as he tries dragging them on an epic hike."

"Well, you just keep standing up for yourself, Korka. You're amazing. Okay, follow me! To my own secret hot spring, which we're *not* going to share with the boys! See you in fifteen minutes, Aron."

Hours later, as Jon is dragging firewood into camp, he sees Leah and Korka wander into sight, giggling and holding hands, their soaking wet hair wrapped in towels. There's no Aron around.

"Where's Aron? You said fifteen minutes. It has been like two hours!" he shouts.

"He's probably not far away, still doing his slingshot practice," Korka says, but there's guilt on her face and in her voice.

"He's eleven," Leah says, "and a very experienced outdoorsman. He's absolutely okay on his own. Cut him more slack, Jon. Korka, too. Maybe he's getting some supper for us. Which would be good, since I see you're empty-handed."

"Did I ask you?"

Jon grabs Korka's arm and pulls her away, lecturing her — yet again — about safety and family rules. Just as he finishes, Aron wanders into camp, whistling. He's swinging two squirrels, dead but not yet stiff, by their tails.

"Yes!" the girls shout. Jon scowls but feels relief overpower his irritation. Food! Never enough, and always welcome.

In fact, there's more food here than they were getting on their own before Leah, and it's much tastier thanks to Leah's spices and cooking skills, which she's busy teaching Korka. Nothing more disappears from the Gunnarssons' packs, and Jon soon finds himself rising each morning to collect wood with Leah, an informal and friendly competition developing.

"Where did you learn to chop wood so fast?" he asks one day, trying to resent her for it.

"None of your ..." Her bright smile contradicts the rudeness of her usual reply.

"Yeah, yeah."

That night he remains by the campfire long after his siblings have roasted the last of Leah's marshmallows and crawled into their tent. His shoulders ache from a hard day's hauling and chopping wood, and he sits on the log seat, hands behind his head, legs extended toward the stone ring around the crackling fire. It's so nice to relax with no responsibilities for a few minutes each day.

Leah places the washed dishes on a towel spread over a stump, then hovers behind him. He can smell her freshly shampooed hair and hear pine cones crunch under her boots as she shifts in place. Then he feels her fingertips push into his shoulder blades and begin to massage them. Electricity runs right down to his toes, and he breathes in deeply, not daring to move for fear she'll take her touch away. And yet, he knows they're crossing into dangerous territory.

After a few minutes, she sits down beside him on the log, a thigh resting against his. He turns and fixes his eyes on her Celtic necklace. He could let things take a romantic course, but he feels a responsibility weighing on him: a need to know who she is, exactly. So, he forces himself to ask softly, "What's your story, really, Leah? Why are your parents looking for you, and why don't you want to be found?"

"Jon, Jon," she says softly, placing a hand on his, her face lit by the flickering flames. "You don't give up, do you?"

"Why would I? You've stolen my family from me. I need to know who you are."

She laughs lightly, like that's a joke. "Okay, but then I get to ask you a few questions. Fair?"

"Fair." He smiles, but her face goes serious.

"The guy who contacted you said he was my father. I don't have a father. I have a stepfather. He's ... a beast."

"What do you mean?"

"Just trust me. My mother doesn't get it, won't believe me, but it wasn't safe living at home anymore. If he hired you to track me down, it's not because he cares about me. Far from it."

"Okay." Jon lets that sink in for a moment. "What about your real father?"

"Not in the picture."

"So, you're going to hide out here from your mother and stepfather forever?"

She goes quiet, and he worries he has shut her down. "That wasn't the original plan," she says eventually. "But it turns out I like it here. Especially since you guys arrived. Why don't you stay, all of you? It's nice sharing the work, don't you think? Korka and Aron seem to be into it. Here's as good as anywhere, isn't it?"

Her tone is soft and seductive, like pine needles drifting to earth. Both her hands are on his now, and he feels the campfire's heat. Everything she says makes sense, and it's not like he hasn't thought about it already. He's tempted to say yes, but he's torn without knowing why.

"I'd have to ask Korka and Aron."

Her laughter is melodic. "They'll say yes, and you know it. It's your decision, Jon. But I think we make a good team."

She rests her head on his shoulder. He doesn't move away.

She sits up again and says slowly, "My turn. What's with Aron hardly ever speaking and being afraid of small spaces?"

Jon bites his tongue. This is not what he expected her to ask. "He's just Aron."

"You're dodging the question."

He studies a wisp of hair that has fallen across her face, and contemplates reaching up and pushing it behind her ear. But she shifts before he gets a chance.

"Okay," she continues. "I know you're teenage runaways, which explains why SAR is after you, but why is this Officer Vine so keen to track you down if he doesn't even like you, and especially doesn't like Aron?"

It's Jon's turn to go quiet a moment. He's starting to regret how much he has told her during their wood-chopping and snare-checking conversations. Too much, clearly.

"It's about saving face. He offered to be our guardian, and we bolted. That makes him look bad in our small community. He's all about law and order, and prestige, and he was always jealous of our family's survival skills, anyway. That's about all I can figure."

"Interesting." She rises to put another log on the fire. Then she turns toward him, still standing.

"There's something else I can't figure out, Jon. If your dad knew so much about survival, how did he get himself in such a bad situation?"

Jon sits bolt upright. "What? Now you're out of bounds, Leah." He struggles to remain calm. "Sorry, but let's not go there."

"Go where?" she asks, sounding overly innocent, as she seats herself beside him again. "What's more curious," she continues, "is why your mom ran out of the house before he was even in trouble."

A current of cold air snakes through the camp and makes him shiver. "No one will ever know," he says quietly, his voice shaking. He desperately wants this conversation to end.

"Okay, sorry." Her voice has gone as gentle as a caress. She reaches out and takes his hands in hers, then leans in, her face close, her eyes exploring his. She smells like spring shoots and fresh air. He knows it's an invitation to kiss her.

So, he's mystified when he shrinks back instead.

The air crackles with tension, and sparks from the fire pop and die.

"Too good for me?" Her tone is icy. "Or is it that you can't control me, like you do poor Korka and Aron?

You're overprotecting them, Jon. And driving them away in the process. You want to drive me away, too?"

"I … I …" He can't figure out what to say, or how to process what just happened.

"Anyway, I answered your questions, and you didn't answer mine." She stands, whirls around, and stalks away. "Good night, Jon." She disappears into the shadows in the direction of her tent.

"Leah, don't —" He wants to go after her, but his boots seem too heavily rooted to the ground.

When she fails to pause or return, he picks up her canvas bucket of water and douses the fire, kicking the wet, black ashes for good measure and hurling the bucket into the bushes. *What did I say wrong this time? Why are girls so difficult?*

He catches a glimpse of Aron's face poking out of the tent flap, spying on him. The kid dares to make a face at Leah's retreating back and give him a thumbs-up.

Huh?

Maybe Aron's right. That was close, too close. We need to get out of here.

NINETEEN

The next morning, before the maidens rise, Aron perches on a log contemplating what he saw the night before. Big Viking is building a teepee of kindling in the cold campfire ring. Aron turns to study a dew-jewelled spiderweb between low-hanging tree branches. He leans forward to get a better look at the large black arachnid that is sitting still and patient in its centre.

"Hungry," Aron says.

"I know. Give me a minute." Jon adds larger sticks to his pyramid, obviously unaware that Aron meant the spider.

Aron is distracted for a moment by the first mosquito he has seen that season. It has bitten his arm, so he slaps it lightly, then picks up its struggling body and plants it in the spider's fiefdom. As soon as Aron withdraws his fingers, the spider scurries thither to lay siege to the morsel. Like a victorious Viking, she wraps up the gift in chain mail–like strands of her web to assure belly timber on the morrow.

Aron pokes Jon in the ribs, determined to get his attention.

"What? I'm busy, Young Viking."

Aron watches a mosquito land on Jon's bare foot, crushes it gently, and picks it up by the wings to place it beside the other injured victim trying to tear itself out of its bonds. A second later, he slaps a third mosquito on his own shoulder and deposits it near the other two victuals. The spider-warrior races like a legendary Nordic hero to roll up these new arrivals, and triumphs in her endeavour.

"Nice," Jon says with a chuckle. "Anyone ever tell you you're a freak, Aron?"

Jon reaches out to tousle Aron's hair, and Aron grabs his brother's wrist and puts his face close to Jon's. He raises three fingers and points to the still-struggling mosquitoes and their busy captor.

"Three," Jon says, a bemused look on his face, clearly not grasping the intended meaning.

Aron points to the spider. "Leah," he says.

Jon's eyes widen and flick back and forth from Aron to the web. A barely perceptible nod means the clan leader has just figured it out, Aron decides, even though he'll need to process and weigh the message now.

"Aron." Leah's commanding voice behind them makes both boys jump. Looking only at Aron, she taps her slingshot. He grabs his reluctantly and follows her thither out of camp, with one parting glance at Jon, who sits staring numbly after them.

Big Viking would follow, Aron senses, but for Leah's accusation the evening before that he is overprotective of his siblings.

Aron wants to tell Leah he doesn't need practice anymore, or further instruction. He's certain she knows that without him even saying it. Plus, looking up at the sky, he realizes that the sunny days they've waited for so long, and enjoyed so briefly, look set to change. Black thunderheads move ominously on the distant horizon, perchance ready to unleash their fury by noontide.

She walks stiffly, briskly, and so far ahead of him that it's like she has forgotten he's in liege with her. He's stumbling and streaming sweat to keep up, like a vassal with too large a girth. He wants to ask her if he's right that the row of small, rounded puffs of grey clouds — cirrostratus — means a severe rainstorm is about to hit.

She strides right past the target tree to a small clearing that feels dark and shadowy. Then she halts and swings around, lowering her face to his. Her voice is gentle, but Aron can feel tension crackling all around her.

"Why are you afraid of small, dark spaces, Aron? Why are you claustrophobic?"

Huh? He stares at her blankly.

"And why do you hardly ever speak?"

He returns her steady gaze, remaining silent even as his pulse picks up like he's besieged.

"They're related, aren't they? Some trauma in childhood?" The words are full of genuine sympathy, but it's like she's talking to herself, not him.

He refuses to respond, but becomes very aware that they're alone, too many leagues from camp for the others to hear them.

"It's something related to Jon, isn't it? He hurt you, didn't he? So, he feels guilty and that makes him overstrict with you. He gets angry when you wander off on your own and tries to make Korka watch you all the time."

Aron shakes his head vigorously while eyeing the tall timber around them, rapidly calculating that he can't outrun or outclimb her if she turns on him.

"My poor Aron." She squats down and tries to put her arms around him, something she has never done before.

He quickly sidesteps away. Despite her warm words, her body feels cold and threatening, like a creature of the shadows.

"You can get past the trauma," she says, and now he knows she's talking to herself again. Maybe *about* herself. "But if Jon's the one who hurt you, you need to get away from him. If you want to run away, Aron, I understand how it is. I can help you. I can protect you."

He shakes his head hard and takes two steps back, his chest pounding. The hurt in her that he sensed when they first met is at full flame, engulfing her. An old wound reopening — maybe because Jon rejected her last night? Prithee she not take it out on him.

"Also, I figure you're not totally claustrophobic or dumb."

Aron winces at her use of the insulting word for a mute person, which she knows he isn't.

"You stayed calm in the bunker when you had to, and you speak when you want to. That means whatever he did to you, it didn't destroy you. You're too strong for that, aren't you, Aron? And you're getting stronger every day here in my camp."

Leah is mixing up her hurt and mine, right?

"You can reverse the damage Jon caused, you know. You just need more practice at speaking, and more time in those tight spaces that scare you. A type of therapy. I can help you."

What? His heartbeat quickens. He calls on the Norse gods to give him strength.

Her left hand reaches out and closes around his wrist, gently but firmly. He pulls but can't break free. Her right hand scoops up a rock on the ground. He flinches and ducks, but it's not a rock she intends to throw at him. It's one that lifts the ground up beside him. Another bunker! A smaller one. A dungeon he does not wish to visit.

"I'll go in with you, and you decide how long we stay. Be brave and see how long you last. Then we'll keep increasing the time until you're okay. Breathe deeply and channel your inner strength, Aron. You need to get over the psychological damage Jon caused. After we come out, tell me what Jon did to you. That's called talk therapy."

"Jon didn't do anything!" he shouts, but the recurring snow cave nightmare that sometimes wakes him begins to play in his head. Was it a real thing that happened, not just a nightmare? But in his dreams, Jon doesn't do anything but save him! And who cares if he doesn't like small spaces?

"Also ..." She pauses for effect. "I think there's something you guys aren't telling me about why your dad had a faulty beacon, and why your mom chased him before he was even in trouble. Is it possible he committed suicide, Aron? Maybe your mother found a note? That's the only thing that makes sense to me."

Aron can't stop the sobs racking his body now.

"I'm so sorry, Aron. I know it's none of my business, and that I'm upsetting you, but I really think facing up to the truth might help all of you."

Aron is trembling and gasping for breath. Is it possible? "Noooo!" he groans. *She doesn't know anything about our parents! How dare she!*

"Because you need to learn to talk, especially about whatever happened. Then you'll be a normal kid, with lots of friends. Not someone hiding in the woods with a warped family. You need to get strong, fight the fear, like I have. Are you listening?"

Hiding, warped family. He knows without a doubt now she's talking about herself, and he feels both sympathy and fear.

As she tries to lead him into the bunker, he makes like a Viking hero, thrashing, applying his super strength, and thrusting his slingshot handle at her like a spear to get away. As he leaves her collapsed in the battle dust, he figures she can hardly hear him blow his emergency whistle for Jon and Korka, because she's weeping herself, a long string of sobs.

And even as he leaves her far behind, a part of him wants to turn back and reach out to comfort this maiden. Because she has been hurt and has no one, while he has a family. A loving, even if argumentative, family of three. And loving parents who died tragically, his father definitely not by choice.

He keeps running and doesn't look behind him.

Back at camp, Korka screams at Jon. "No! I'm not leaving! I like it here! Leah's way nicer than you! We don't need to go anywhere. We can just stay here!"

"Korka." Jon never expected this to be easy. His sister has gotten way too attached to Leah. They all have. She has woven them into her web. And she has her own issues, stuff they can't help her with in their own fragile state.

"Even when you turn eighteen," Korka shouts, "I don't want to live with you, and Aron probably doesn't either, so there! We're staying!"

"Aron does not want to stay. He told me this morning that ... that he has a bad feeling about Leah," Jon says. "Not in so many words. But it's what he meant."

"Bull! You're making that up! He'd never say that about Leah!"

Jon turns and starts packing up the items in their tent, then the tent itself, and finally the empty food bag, which he stuffs into the top of his pack. Korka stands with arms crossed, face puckered like she's fighting tears. Jon lines up their packs like they're expecting a curbside taxi pickup.

"Go ask Aron yourself," Jon says. "Not that he should be out of your sight, anyway. I'm telling you it's time to go. And I'm the leader."

She's opening her mouth to reply when they hear blasts of a whistle. They both tense, look about, and try to determine the source of the sound. Minutes later, Aron comes sprinting into camp, his grimy hands wiping tears from his dirt-covered face. He runs into Jon's arms and presses himself against his ribs with a ferocity Jon has never felt.

Jon tenses and reaches for the weapons on his belt, but he sees nothing or no one in pursuit. He squats down and hugs his brother tight.

"Aron, Aron? Are you okay?"

Aron leans up to whisper in his ear so quietly that Jon barely hears him. "Did Dad commit suicide? Did he leave a note that Mom found? Is that why she ran after him before he was in trouble?"

"No!" Jon says, horrified. *No way! Dad would never.* He wraps Aron in his strong arms again. "Is that what Leah —"

They're interrupted by Leah walking into camp, slingshot jammed in her pocket. She fixes all three and their packed gear in her gaze.

"You're leaving?" She sounds devastated but not surprised.

Jon is torn and totally confused. He has no idea how Aron got the suicide theory into his head, whether it even came from Leah, or what else she may have done to upset him. But he's not about to repeat Aron's chilling questions in front of Korka.

He stands and tries to pull himself together. As much as he wants to stay, he knows this moment has been coming, and he has rarely seen Aron so strong-willed.

"Thank you for all you've done," he says as neutrally as he can, backing up a step, "but we're leaving, Leah, all three of us." He releases Aron, who immediately runs to Korka and clings to her.

Korka gazes at Leah, disbelief on her face. "What have you done to my brother?"

"Nothing. I was trying to help him with his claustrophobia."

"What?" Korka asks sharply, looking from Leah to Aron. She hugs Aron harder.

"And he was about to tell me the truth of what happened to your parents."

"They died in an avalanche! An accident." Jon's voice has gone deep, thanks to the constriction in his chest.

"She didn't hurt me," Aron says, then adds, "but it's time to go."

Jon stares at Leah. What happened between her and Aron? Leah somehow looks in need of comforting, but Aron is the one with good instincts.

"You two don't have to leave with Jon," Leah says to Korka, voice sweet as wild clover. "Anyway, it's dangerous to go now. There's a storm coming."

"Did something happen?" Korka asks Aron.

Jon watches Aron's arms tighten around her. Korka leans down and, in one strong swoop, shoulders her backpack. Aron promptly slides into his pack and then hangs tightly onto her hand. Jon throws Leah an apologetic look and grabs the rest of their gear.

"Goodbye, Leah," Korka says stiffly, sadly, face full of confusion. "Thanks for … everything."

"Um, bye, Leah. For now," Jon says. "Maybe we'll run into each other again some day? Take care of yourself," he adds, voice cracking as he turns away.

Jon leads the way, boots dragging, and the three march wordlessly into the blackening forest. His heart is a bundle of pain as he struggles to ignore the frantic stream of words behind them: *forgive me*, and *please stay*, and then a resigned *good luck*.

TWENTY

They survive the storm by staking down their tent at dusk and leaping inside just as the clouds burst above them and rain pelts down. Streams of water pour down the tent sides in a steady rhythm as sheet lightning freeze-frames their limp forms slumped on the bedding inside. Thunder rattles their shelter and their bones, and no one makes a move to do chores or prepare supper, especially since there is no food or fuel.

"Thor, god of thunder, is our friend," Aron says, his first words since they left Leah's camp.

Jon manages a smile for his brother.

"Aron?" Korka says, tentatively.

Aron turns her way slowly — slowly and reluctantly, Jon notes. "Did she ... hurt you?"

Silence. Then, "No. Scared me. But she didn't mean to."

"Can you tell us what happened?" Jon coaxes.

Silence. Then, "I like not talking."

"You mean you don't want to tell us anything?" Jon asks, disappointment flooding him.

"No, I mean I like not talking much. It's just me. And lots of Viking kids are claustrophobic."

In the shadows, Jon sees Korka's eyebrows rise. His own breathing quickens.

"The snow cave collapse was just nature," Aron continues. "Nature after I did something stupid. It's no one's fault. It was never your fault, Jon."

Jon is astonished. Aron remembers the snow cave incident? And even so, Aron is forgiving him?

"You remember the snow cave?" Korka asks Aron, sounding amazed.

"*You* remember it?" Jon asks her.

"Of course," she says. "And he's right. It wasn't anyone's fault."

Jon reaches out to squeeze Aron's shoulder, his eyes smarting. "I led us there."

"But you were young, too. We followed. And you rescued us," Aron says. "Not your fault. And I don't want to talk about Leah anymore." He buries his face in his sleeping bag.

Jon watches Korka sink down slowly and pull her sleeping bag up to her chin, choosing for once to say nothing. Maybe at a loss for words, like Jon is.

He draws in a big, deep breath. A pulse pounds in his head. So, maybe the snow cave collapse wasn't the cause or beginning of Aron's claustrophobia or ... his being Aron. Of his choosing to speak only when he has to, wants to, and mostly only to family. Or if it was, it doesn't matter. It never has. Jon doesn't need to carry that burden anymore.

He lies with his hands behind his head, staring at the roof of the tent as rain pounds it. Hearing the eventual heavy breathing of his tentmates, he feels relieved. He'll ask Aron about the suicide notion another time, when Korka is not around.

They're close beside him, his charges. Safe and sound. The day of the snow cave disaster, he led them into danger. But he also led them out of it, it's true. And he's doing so again now. They're a threesome again. Weak and short of food, but surviving. Where on earth do they go from here?

To the mining village, of course. Having studied the map, he's calculated it's a two-day hike, and even if they find no berries on the way, he thinks they're strong enough to make that.

The next morning in the fresh, rain-cleansed air, Jon doles out a tablespoon of oatmeal each, which finishes the very last of their food. They each trickle water over it, fantasize about sugar and milk and cinnamon and a spoonful of nuts, and let it excite their taste buds for a moment before swallowing.

"Two days of walking, if we hardly stop except for the night," Jon tells them.

No one objects. There are no meals to stop for, and no one seems to have the energy to hunt. They keep close together, pausing only to drink copious amounts of purified water and rub cramps from their calves.

Aron follows close behind Jon and Korka, doubling his pace if they get so much as two steps away. At night, he seems to welcome his sister's arms around him and the kisses Jon plants on his head.

Jon's stomach feels raw, tight, and empty, his energy seeping away. He figures it's the same for his siblings, but they don't complain. Aron shows no interest in pulling out his slingshot, nor do Jon or Korka ever slow their pace enough to set snares or fish. Each one knows it's an all-or-nothing march to the ghost town and its store beyond.

The second morning, before Aron stirs, Korka whispers to Jon, "What do you think Leah did to Aron? And what did she mean by 'the truth' about our parents?"

"Shh," Jon replies. "He said she didn't hurt him."

He's relieved when she backs off, perhaps for fear Aron will wake and listen in.

"Think she'll follow us, or report us?"

Jon thinks about it for a moment, then replies with a definitive no. He wants to add that, after his birthday, when they've sorted out their own family, he wants to go back and find Leah to see if she'll let him assist her. She helped them, and the bond the three of them formed with her doesn't need to be broken. Right?

He turns over and falls back asleep, until a little later when his siblings tug him out of the tent by the end of his sleeping bag.

"Gotta go, Big Viking. No slackers in this clan. Tent needs packing," Korka teases him.

That day, they achieve only half the distance of the day before. Their feet drag, and their packs feel like they've doubled in weight even without food. They're a trio of sleepwalkers in dire need of sustenance. On steep uphills, they barely stumble forward.

When the body runs out of reserves of fat to supply energy, Jon recalls reading, it begins to break down muscle and tissue to supply its energy needs. This can rapidly lead to death.

"Jon!" Korka shouts sometime that afternoon.

Jon whirls around. Aron has stumbled and is sitting down, stringy arms hugging his knees, glassy eyes staring forward.

"Aron." Jon reaches for his hand. "Not much farther. You've been doing so well. You can do the final bit, Little Viking."

Instead of rising, Aron slumps the rest of the way to the ground. "Can't," he rasps, eyes closing. He rolls over onto his side.

"Has he fainted?" Korka sinks to the earth beside him and cups her hands around his face.

Jon squats beside his brother. Leave it to Aron to collapse before it occurs to him to complain.

"Can we rest?" Korka asks. "Is there anything else to eat at all, some emergency granola bar or something?" She looks at Jon with dull but hopeful eyes, and he wishes with all his heart he'd held something back for this moment.

"Sorry," he whispers, touching her head.

She swats his hand away and bends forward, her thin shoulders trembling. "I can't go any farther, either."

Aron has opened his eyes. He spots a line of ants and scoops up a few to put in his mouth. Swallows them. Jon shudders but doesn't stop him.

"Ugh," Korka says, covering her eyes. Then she adds curiously, "What do they taste like?"

"Vinegar," Aron says.

"I've been eating my lip balm," she admits. "It tastes like strawberries."

Jon stares up at the towering trees and feels imprisoned by their swaying forms. He could lie down right here and sleep forever, but he's the leader, so he rises shakily to his feet.

"I'll just hike to that rise and see what's ahead." He lifts his water bottle to his mouth and takes a couple deep swigs.

He has staggered forward for about ten minutes when the trail nears a cliff offering a sweeping view. One glimpse of the valley below brings tears of relief. He run-walks back to his crew with newfound energy.

"The mining town! It's just below us! I've seen it!"

Korka gives him a tired smile, stands up slowly, and shrugs back into her pack.

You can do it, son, Jon imagines his father saying, a loving grip on his shoulder. *You're strong and determined.* Warmth radiates through his body. He never, ever imagined such warmth could be snatched away from him. They *need* their parents. Hot tears threaten.

Aron doesn't move.

"Aron?" Jon asks, hovering over him worriedly.

"Can't. Sorry," he whispers.

"Yes, you can!" Jon leans down and wills himself the strength to lift Aron off the ground, to swing him up and over his shoulders and hold him like a sack. "We're a team, Aron. Three, remember? I'll carry you all the way, if I have to."

"Odin endured," Aron mumbles weakly, quoting from who knows where.

"Odin endured three hardships in his quest for the runes," Korka finishes for him softly. "Runes were magical charms for protection and healing."

There's no answer. Aron has fallen asleep on Jon's shoulder.

"I think we've endured more than three hardships," Jon says. "And I don't know about you, but I think we three Vikings have earned some protection and healing." As they work their way down the stony trail, Jon picking his way carefully, he adds, "Korka, please don't be disappointed if the buildings are in terrible condition. All we're really looking for is —"

"— a place to stay till you turn eighteen," she says quietly.

Jon nods and says nothing more.

It's a long march down into the valley. At one point, Aron revives enough to stumble along between them, supported by both. *We're a team*, Jon says to himself.

"Yes!" Korka shouts when they finally reach the cluster of rickety wood cabins beside an ambling stream. A dozen shacks, if you count the two whose roofs have fallen in. In a green space surrounded by snow-capped mountains. To the far right of the shacks are the scattered remains of a mining operation: ragged steel drums, cracked wheels and cogs, old mining carts, pipes, coils of wire, and rusty rails to nowhere.

Jon lays Aron down on a sagging porch and coaxes him to drink from his water bottle. Then he joins Korka, who is moving up and down the row of huts, dashing in to open cupboards in case they hold forgotten tins of food. But no such luck.

The simple huts are so close together that the miners could have shaken hands from the side windows. If there were ever any picket fences, vagrants have long since nabbed them for firewood to feed a giant blackened fire-pit beside the last shelter, which Jon is concerned looks like a party destination.

This last cabin's aged wooden floor is covered in broken glass bottles and empty beer cans, a vintage ice chest with a burn hole in it, and two camping chairs with legs missing. Mouldy hammocks are strung from hooks in the walls. When Jon kicks a pile of garbage bags in one corner, a fat rat scurries out and runs between his legs, and maggots fall squirming from the hole in the plastic. So, someone was here not so long ago.

"Not this one." Korka covers her nose and mouth and backs up.

They recheck the other huts one by one, finding a chair here, a stool there, and garbage everywhere. One hut offers up a yellowed wall calendar from 1966. Two have old barrels that must once have held water. Some have rotted floorboards they have to be careful not to fall through.

As they work their way back to the first cabin, Jon points to its broken windows.

"Who cares about the windows? This is the one!" Korka enthuses, her smile spreading as she points to torn lace curtains hanging askew.

It's the largest shack, Jon notes, perhaps the manager's house. It was once red, judging from the peeling paint. They walk up its two warped front steps and go inside, where they find built-in, hand-hewn bunkbeds without mattresses and a set of bedsprings leaning against the wall.

"Three beds!" Aron says, revived enough to peek in.

"You're being pretty generous with your definition of beds, Aron," Jon says sourly.

There's a pot-bellied iron stove disconnected from the wall, and a stick broom below one of the two broken windows. In the corner stands a cupboard whose warped door Jon manages to pry open. Inside are sawdust, dead wasps and ants, and a jumbo, unopened can of chili.

"Food!" cries Aron. He bolts in to grab it from Jon.

"Not so fast," Jon says, lifting it out of Aron's reach and inspecting the lid and bottom. He flicks off rust from both ends and sets the can down. "Sorry. We don't need food poisoning."

As Korka picks up the broom to sweep and Jon hauls the rusty bedsprings and some garbage to the dump established beside the farthest cabin, Aron wanders behind the cabins, through a patch of weeds and wildflowers and toward the stream.

"Fish!" Jon hears him call out a moment later. Aron returns and the two unearth the fishing line from Jon's pack.

As he stands by the stream watching Aron work the line, Jon takes in the sun glinting off the tumbling water. The moving fish seem to wink at him. It takes Aron only half an hour to haul in four fish.

They're out of camp stove fuel and too hungry and nervous about being detected to build a fire outside, so they vote to eat the fish raw. Four bony mountain white-fish don't go far in three shrunken stomachs, but eating anything at all, especially stuffed with the edible wild-flowers that Korka has gathered from the clearing, rates as a welcome feast.

With slightly renewed energy, they collect pieces of broken furniture from the other cabins, transfer legs from some pieces onto others with duct tape and wire from Jon's pack, and soon have created a livable area. Jon secures the tent over the hole in the roof, Korka fetches water from the stream and purifies it, and Aron arranges the sleeping bags and pads: his and Korka's on the bunkbeds, Jon's on a pile of evergreen boughs he has hauled in and arranged on the freshly swept floor under the window.

It's not much, but it's a space to call their own.

TWENTY-ONE

As night falls, Jon knows the other two are waiting for him to bring up the million-dollar question.

"Who wants to join me on the hike into Wolfsburg?" he finally asks. "It's over a snowy pass, a two-day walk if we push it hard and if the weather and snow conditions co-operate."

He watches Korka and Aron gaze out the back window, where the sun's last rays cast a glow on the wildflowers, quiet forest, and tumbling stream. Water gurgles over the rocks, an owl hoots, and a chorus of crickets is accompanied by frogs croaking in rhythmic bass.

"You'll travel a lot faster without Aron and me," Korka says. "I'm not even sure the two of us could make it. Plus it's safer with just you, if people are looking for three runaways. We'll be okay here on our own, and you won't be long. It's spring now. Aron and I can find some birds' nests and catch more fish."

Jon heaves a sigh, having expected this reply. He has sworn never to leave them alone, but this situation calls for an exception.

"It's a full day's hike to the summit, then a short trip down to Wolfsburg," he says. "Up on the pass, there's a cave on the right just off the trail. It's a five-minute walk above where you see three alpine firs joined together at the trunk. Dad and I stayed in that cave one night in a freak spring snowstorm. You need to know in case any visitors show up here, or in case of an emergency. But like I said, it'll take you a full day to get there, so you'd need to start in the early morning."

Aron nods soberly. Then he turns. "Why three trees on one trunk?"

Jon smiles tiredly as he recalls asking his father that same question the night they trudged to the cave. The memory warms him, so he recites his father's answer. "In a forest, trees grow toward the sky, reaching for whatever light they can get. Some tree species have a 'leader' that keeps that role by chemically suppressing side branches from reaching higher. But trauma can turn a single tree into one that shares its trunk with others. Beavers, flooding, or fire temporarily halt growth, and then the tree suddenly rebounds with a twin."

"Or triplets," Aron says with a yawn.

"Yeah. Multi-trunk trees are kind of cool, and this one makes it easy to find the cave," Jon says.

Korka fingers the crocheted-cord necklace that Leah gave her, lifts it off her neck, and presents it to Jon. "Protection," she says, and gives him a rare hug. "By the way, I want to apologize for not listening to you the day I fell and sprained my ankle. It was my fault … for being stubborn."

"Thanks, Korka. We've all learned a lot since then." He returns the embrace fiercely, then cups Aron's head in his hands and kisses his brother's forehead. "Take care of each other. I'll leave before you're even awake in the morning."

As he pulls away, his heart skips a beat. He's actually going to leave these two alone for three days? With no one to protect them if nasty hikers or a dangerous animal shows up? Then again, if he had to pick two children from anywhere in the world to fend for themselves in this valley, these are the two he would most trust.

He lies down on the bough bed Aron made for him, feeling squeezed by worry even as he tries to persuade himself that what he is doing is right.

"Before you go," Korka says, rising slowly from her bunkbed and standing over his prone form, "you or Aron have to tell me what Leah meant when she said, 'the truth of what happened to your parents.'"

He tenses. "Leave it," he responds, adding, "please." But that just makes Korka put her face in his.

"Tell her," Aron says from the top bunk, his voice surprisingly commanding. "What I told you Leah said to me."

Jon and Korka turn to Aron, startled.

"So, it was Leah?" Jon asks. "She didn't know what she was talking about. It was very, very cruel to say it to you. She may have taken a survival course from Mom and Dad, but she *didn't know them*."

"*What* was cruel? *What* did Leah say?" Korka shouts into the darkening cabin.

"Dad didn't," Aron says, tears starting.

"He didn't," Jon assures him, trying to figure out how to calm Korka down.

"Dad didn't what?" Korka shrieks.

"Leah said Mom ran because —" Aron chokes out.

"She ran because she trusted your gut feeling," Jon says, rising from his bed and moving to embrace his little brother. "You had a premonition. You suspected it before it happened. You and your psychic brain. That's why you tried to stop Dad from leaving, which upset Mom. A few minutes later, she decided to act on it."

Korka stands there with jaw lowered, apparently speechless and trying to form her next words. Before she can say anything, Jon feels an unexpected bitterness erupt in his soul.

"But, Aron, you didn't tell *us*. *We* could have stopped him."

Aron twists into a ball in his bunk and puts his hands over his ears.

"You heard me! *We* could have stopped him if you hadn't kept it to yourself! Your clinging to him didn't actually save him, did it? Nor did it save Mom, who might not have run after him if you hadn't scared her!"

"There wasn't a suicide note. He didn't." Aron sobs. "I'm sorry! I'm sorry!"

"Suicide note?" Korka screams.

Now Jon is holding his head in his hands. "I'm sorry, sorry, sorry, Aron! It wasn't your fault! It was mine for not helping more with the money stuff!"

The entire bunk is shuddering with Aron's sobbing. Korka's head jerks from one to the other in a frantic haze, like she's torn between comforting Aron and pummelling Jon. Instead, she grabs her headlamp and runs out of the cabin, bare feet on broken glass, hands over her ears.

Jon finds her curled into a ball on the cold ground, hitting the dirt with her fists.

"Noooo!" Korka screeches into the night. Her cry silences the crickets, frogs, owl, and wind.

He wraps himself around her. "I'm sorry, Korka. I shouldn't have shouted at Aron. I just apologized to him. And Leah's going to totally get it from me for suggesting Dad might have —"

"There's no way he did! How dare Leah even think it!"

"But I need to explain something you don't know. Mom and Dad were in lots of debt."

"I know that!"

"You do? How?"

"I'm not as dumb as you think."

"It's my fault for not helping them more," he says, choking on the words. "I think the money stuff made Dad stressed and distracted those last weeks. I think that's why he didn't check the batteries on his beacon."

203

She regards him through squinted eyes. "You could've helped them more. You were always sneaking off to your room to study for the EMT test and lying to them that you were doing your homework, when you could've helped them."

"I know." His voice cracks. "Then Aron had some kind of premonition that morning."

"Like I hadn't already figured that out."

"And the way he clung to Dad, then Mom, it spooked her, so she —"

"— chased after him. Jon, Dad's death is not your fault. And it's not Aron's."

He feels his heart crumple. "Leah thought it added up to suicide, maybe because I told her Dad was stressed by the debt stuff. She decided that maybe Mom had found a note, and that's why she ran out before he even skied off the … and Leah asked Aron if it might be true."

"So, that's why he was upset and wanted to get away from her."

"That, and she was trying to get him to spend time in a bunker with her, to 'cure' him. He told me yesterday."

"What? Leah? I don't believe it!"

"Aron insists she did it nicely, and meant well." A stab of guilt hits him for leaving Leah there, abruptly and alone, as she begged forgiveness.

"Meant well?" Korka sounds as dumbfounded as Jon was when Aron first said it. "Okay, maybe. She's not cruel or crazy that I ever saw."

"Uh-huh."

"But she actually s-said the word *s-suicide* to Aron?" Korka asks between choking sobs.

"It was mean, but she didn't intend it to be. She's dealing with her own issues."

"You *knew* Leah asked Aron if it was suicide? Why didn't you tell me?"

"I never got the chance," Jon says. "And I didn't want to upset you."

"You had no right to hide that. You think you're so far above me you can't be honest, can't share important info and plan together? This whole trip, you've been obsessed with being the boss of us. You don't even know what a team is. Bet you'd never, ever use your whistle to ask *us* to help *you*. And you *actually* just blamed Aron just for not warning us when he freaked out on Mom and Dad? He's in that cabin all alone now, blaming himself and reliving the avalanche nightmare all over again."

"We'll go back in a second. You deserve to be angry, Korka," Jon says calmly. "But tomorrow I'll go to Wolfsburg and bring back food and fuel, and we'll all get strong again, and then we'll be okay."

"It's cold out here," Aron says from behind them.

Jon bites his tongue. They should've known he'd follow them outside and listen. Jon rises, takes both his siblings' hands, and leads them back into the bunkhouse. There, he helps them into their sleeping bags, which he pulls up to their chins before kissing them good night.

"I'm sorry," Jon says again in a broken voice.

"We're all sorry," Korka says.

He turns to the wall and swallows a salty tear. An image thrusts itself into his mind: Aron hanging on to their father in the hall moments before he left. Then a searing slow-mo replay of his strong, capable, loving father stepping off the cornice, the snow thundering down, then of their distraught mother giving chase. The sequence leaps suddenly to Leah confessing why she was hiding in the woods, about her beast of a stepfather. Now she's alone again, after sharing so many skills and so much time with them. She's got to be crazy lonely since they turned their backs on her. And he misses her.

"I'm going to be the boss now," Jon hears Korka say to Aron. "I'll protect you till Jon gets back."

TWENTY-TWO

The next morning Korka wakens at a touch to her forehead. Aron is standing over her, holding out two open palms piled with luscious-looking blueberries. She must be dreaming. She sits up so fast that she bumps her head on the bottom of the upper bunk. He's real, her smiling brother. Her body tingles as she stares at the food.

Then she takes a quick look around. Jon's bed is empty, his pack gone. Almost all its contents are in a pile by the foot of his bed. From the look of things, he has taken nothing but his sleeping bag, water bottle, flashlight, knife, money, aspirin, and whistle. Leaving Aron

PAM WITHERS

and her all the essentials. Gambling his life on what's left of his strength. He hadn't even rested or eaten more than last night's scraggly fish. Never mind that he's a living skeleton, like them.

A rush of memories, guilt, and distress hit her like a collapsing roof. She was vicious to him last night, beyond anything she could apologize for now.

"They're ripe," Aron is saying. "From a patch of blueberry bushes just across the stream."

Her mouth waters despite her distress. She takes some of the berries in her grimy fingers and pushes them between her dry lips. Her taste buds all but explode with pleasure. She wants to grab Aron's hands and pour all the berries into her mouth. She wants to run to the patch to pluck and seize every morsel of the blue fruit until her belly screams *stop*. She has never known such hunger.

"You're the best, Aron."

He grins wider. She accepts the blueberries and forces herself to suck on them slowly and swallow one at a time. Of course the miners would have pruned and harvested wild blueberry bushes near their little community — a patch no doubt overgrown by now but still producing.

Glancing out the window, she sees by the sun that it's almost midday.

"Found this in the dump pile," Aron adds, holding up a piece of screen almost the same size as him. "We can fish with it."

She pictures the two of them placing the screen across the narrow river, trapping gobs of fish. "Genius," she says.

Food. Above all, they need food and rest. They'll have plenty of both here. Jon should have stayed till he was stronger. But she failed to suggest that. Instead, she drove him away.

She covers her face with her hands, but Aron places his over hers and lifts them away. He leads her outside into the sunshine.

By late afternoon, they've used one of the packs to haul their sleeping bags and pads across the stream so they can lounge in the warm sun, a pot of blueberries by their side, the skeletons of fish littered about them. Aron's using his slingshot to lob stones into tree trunks. Korka's Swiss Army knife, smelling of fish guts, lies by her. She's playing with the compass to pass the time. They are full and content, the fullest and most content they've been on this trip, Korka reflects.

But as shadows fall and the orange sun eases toward the far horizon, the sound of singing and shouting reaches their ears. Korka and Aron both leap up. Instantly, they head for some thick brush with their gear in tow.

"Wahoo! Someone left us stuff!" a deep male voice shouts from their cabin, and Korka hears thumps of gear flying against walls. "A folding saw! A camp stove and flint! A snare! A tent!" They list off more finds. "We've hit the jackpot, guys!"

Korka lunges up, temper boiling, but Aron grabs her arm to restrain her. With effort, she drops back down. Aron's right, she realizes. Better to see how many of them there are, or wait till nighttime to retrieve their stuff.

"Eight," Aron whispers a few minutes later, and she agrees as she counts the figures gathering in the dusk.

All the guys look a little older than Jon. Some of them are covered in tattoos, and all of them are swaggering with open cans of beer in their hands. Several begin building a fire — as in a seriously big bonfire with wood they're chopping from nearby trees — in the firepit near the farthest cabin. Her body is all tensed up, disappointment rippling through her. This was supposed to be their quiet, safe place. Their new home. How dare a bunch of losers shows up.

"We'll sleep here tonight," she whispers, tapping their sleeping bags where they're hidden in a thicket. "Maybe they'll leave tomorrow."

It's the smell of hot dogs a few hours later that messes with her mind. It's dark, the guys' fire is roaring, and they're bellowing with laughter as rap music blasts endless four-letter words from a speaker. Two are wrestling dangerously close to the fire. And someone is attempting to play a poorly tuned guitar. A few are crawling into sagging tents they've set up near the fire.

These are not experienced backcountry people, she thinks, though they obviously made it over a pass. But they have food. Real food. Her stomach, awakened by the blueberries and fish, is ravenous for their grub.

She checks that Aron is sleeping, then crawls on hands and knees toward the smell. It drags her forward like a long grasping arm. She crosses the stream and detours to Aron's and her cabin, only to find all their gear gone. Her fists clench. Minutes later, she's close enough to their unwanted visitors to see firelight reflected on their ugly faces. Close enough to see a full bag of hot dogs and another of buns sitting on a log well behind the wannabe guitar player.

They're trying to sing to the rap. Pathetic. She waits till their voices crescendo, their heads lifted to the moon like howling wolves.

With one smooth grab, she snatches the bags. Then she's running, triumphant at liberating days' worth of sustenance from the party site. Until she feels a fist grab the hood of her sweatshirt and yank her off her feet. The bags of food go flying, and she lands with a painful thump on the ground.

"What do we have here?" slurs a deep voice.

She struggles to loosen herself from his grip, but he lifts her up off the ground like she's a six pack of empties and carries her to the fire, where he seats her on a log, his steely arm encircling her waist.

"Dudes! We got a chick come to party with us! Anyone else with ya?" he asks, peering into the dark behind her. "Or are you all mine?"

He pushes his pimply face close to hers, his beery breath invading her nostrils. The others gather around, hooting and hollering, one of them pulling her up and grabbing her buttocks with his big hand.

She's about to pull a defence move on them when the big guy beside her pulls her away from the others.

"Hungry, are you? Thirsty, too, I bet. Dudes! Bring my girlfriend some hot dogs and beer! Underage for drinking, maybe, but dying for one, anyway, right?"

Too many to fight all at once. Better to play their game.

"Hey, glad you guys rolled in," she says in the bravest voice she can muster. "I was getting lonely camped here all by myself. And I'm starved. If you have some food I can eat before the beer, please. I'm Cora. What're your names?" She directs a glowing and hopefully not-too-shaky smile at the muscle-bound guy beside her.

"I'm Bud," he says. "We're all from Wolfsburg. Hey, Cora, you out here all on your own? That's so cool. Are you a party girl?"

"Totally!" she says with enthusiasm into his grizzled face and bleary eyes, trying desperately to keep fear and loathing out of hers. She slips a moist hand into his large one, at the same time sizing him up from head to toe.

Someone else, the only cute guy, pushes a paper plate her way. "Hey, thanks!" she says, her enthusiasm genuine this time. "Aww, only one hot dog? I'm totally starved, you know. Need energy to hang out with you all."

"Bring the princess another plate!" someone shouts.

With all the concentration she can summon, she eats slowly, politely, rather than shoving down the dogs and potato salad and potato chips and chocolate-chip cookies the way her raging appetite urges her to. She also fervently hopes Aron stays asleep where she left him, that he won't find her gone and try doing something dumb.

The camp food joins the blueberries and fish, and it all churns around in gurgling discomfort. That gives her an idea. She reaches for the beer that Bud offers her, toasts them all, and takes a long pretend swig. Then she pastes a stricken look on her face, covers her mouth with her hand, and with high drama, says, "Uh-oh."

She rises from the log, dashes behind the nearest cabin, and makes loud vomiting sounds. The whole crowd jeers: "Ha! A lightweight! Euuww! Puke baby. You can kiss 'er first, Bud."

While they're still laughing, she sprints in the dark to the stream. She's about to splash into it and cross to the other side, when someone, Cute Guy, grabs her from behind. She raises the side of her right wrist, carefully keeping her arm at a right angle to create space between her and her attacker. Then she twists her knee to connect with his groin, and down he goes. The guy behind him shouts the F-word as slingshot rocks hit him, *smack, smack, smack.*

Aron's across the stream helping her!

Then she's across the cold creek, free, running, running uphill through trees in pale starlight, Aron on her heels, his panting resounding in her ears. He turns around at intervals to lob another rock or two.

The two pause just long enough to grab their sleeping bags, pads, and backpack, and then plunge into the dark forest, as nimble now as mountain goats, as silent as ghosts.

"We're okay," she finally whispers, knowing the bullies won't chase them far in the dark, though adrenalin courses through her. They sink to the ground. "Thanks, Aron. We'll sleep here and move on first thing in the morning."

It's pitch black. She can't see where they are, but she hears Aron climbing up a tree beside her and glimpses his outline tying his sleeping bag's stuff sack between two branches, like he's bear-proofing food supplies. "What're you doing?"

"Protecting the hot dogs and buns you stole. I followed you across the stream and got them without those guys seeing me."

"Of course you did." She smiles.

"I ate three."

"Hmm, three."

"What about our stuff in the cabin?" he asks, returning to her side.

"Gone. But we don't need stuff," she declares. "We're survival experts."

"Okay. But even Viking magnates need sleeping bags and a compass."

"Which we have, along with a Swiss Army knife, a slingshot, and one empty pack."

They crawl into their sleeping bags in the night's warmish air. She reaches through the dark to touch Aron's shoulders, needing his small, calm form to soothe her still-electrified nerves. Her heartbeat gradually slows.

Bastards. How dare they. But she showed them. She and Aron together.

She can't fall asleep. The grinding beat of the rap and glow of the bonfire are not far enough away. Plus, the fire is growing, billowing higher. And it smells like —

She bolts upright, sniffs again. "Aron."

He's up the nearest tree like a shot, scouting the site. Shouting reaches their ears.

"The last cabin is on fire," Aron reports. She clambers up the tree to a lower branch to see for herself.

"Idiots!" she says. "The shacks are so close together, they'll all go up."

Even as she says this, flames leap from the roof of the last cabin to the next structure. Loud crackles and crashes filter up to the two hidden observers as the first cabin to catch fire caves in. Korka sees figures standing to one side, probably half-shocked, half-delighted. Maybe they started it on purpose. The tents have been dragged to safety, and the guys are tossing things into the fast-expanding fire and laughing.

Over the next hour, the rest of the cabins catch fire and cave in, adding fuel to the flames that reach higher and higher into the night sky. The sobered-up partyers have formed a fire brigade now, extending from stream to the housing row. They're passing containers of water from one to the other, dampening the ground around so the fire doesn't spread to the forest.

"Should we go down and help?" Aron asks.

"Not in my lifetime," she says, pursing her lips. A historic mining village is disappearing before their eyes, she reflects sadly. It was abandoned for too long — a party destination once too often.

"We'll hike up to the cave in the pass tomorrow, first thing. Jon will find us there." She reaches for Aron and holds him close. They gaze up at the stars through the drifting smoke, which in time begins to thin.

Feeling calmer now, Korka says, "Good night, Aron. Thanks for rescuing me tonight."

"Was fun."

"You're my hero."

"Pretty brave yourself," he replies, gazing up at the bag of bear-proofed hot dogs. "And stupid."

"Yup."

A moment's silence, then, "I miss Jon," he says.

"Me, too."

TWENTY-THREE

All night in the cave, Jon is bombarded by memories of sleeping there during that storm several years before. He remembers the calming presence of his strong, in-charge father. The storytelling they did by candlelight to keep each other entertained as a howling wind whipped heavy snow around outside. He recalls the clouds of breath they emitted together, and how they laughed and pretended they were cartoon speech bubbles.

In the morning, he was nervous when they stepped outside the cave onto so much new-fallen snow, worried that the avalanche chute between them and the downward slope to Wolfsburg looked unstable. But his dad simply handed him a shovel, made him do his snow-pit test, and nodded proudly when he ruled it was okay to cross the couloir — the narrow, steep gully on the mountain, walled in by more or less vertical cliffs.

The memories are as strong as the damp cave walls, and they only serve to make the place more starkly lonely. Was it right to leave his siblings in the ghost town and promise to return, the way his mother had promised to return when she dashed out after their father? Who does he think he is, so certain of returning with food and fuel after climbing up and down a mountain pass twice, in his condition?

But he's the oldest, the leader.

So proud of you, son. Keep an eye on your siblings. Some of his father's last words.

As dawn offers weak light, he listens to the drip, drip, drip of water leaking into the cave through cracks in the ceiling, and he lifts his empty water bottle up to collect them, knowing it's a risk. He left the purification tablets and cooking pan with his siblings, but he isn't about to put time or energy into building a fire from scratch to boil snow. Next, he stuffs his sleeping bag in his pack and staggers out of the rock shelter, stiff and chilled as a half-frozen carcass.

He can hardly tell it's morning. A heavy fog is rolling in. And he left the compass back at the ghost town. He'd rather Korka and Aron have it in the unlikely event of an emergency. Anyway, for now he can see snatches of tiny Wolfsburg far below, between the low drifting puffs of cloud, and that lifts his spirits.

The cave is two-thirds of the way from the mining town to Wolfsburg. He's closer to town than to where he's come from. He's weak and tired but determined to reach it at any cost, maybe even get back to the cave tonight. He imagines his father beside him. *We can do this, Big Viking. We're tough as bark.*

Sure, Dad. He smiles. Hmm, bark.

He tries to get used to seeing snow again, up here in this pass. Such a contrast to the velvety green valley be-low. He slides down from the cave to the three alpine fir trees growing out of a single massive trunk. Reaching up to one of them, he uses his knife to slice off a strip, vertical and narrow to make sure he inflicts as little damage to the tree as possible. Next, with blade and dirty fingernails, he separates the hard part of the bark from the soft part and stuffs pieces of the hard bark into his parka pocket. He chews the soft bits, the cambium tissue, like he's training for a jaw-muscle-strength competition, then spits out the stringy remains with all the gusto of a tobacco chewer.

"To you, Mom and Dad," he says, toasting them as he completes his breakfast. "It's not gourmet, but it's calories."

Knowing he's at the edge of the avalanche zone, he kneels down and paws at the snow to create a snow pit that would barely pass muster in his parents' course. Then tries removing a straight-edged block from it. *Yeah, well, I don't have a saw. I have to make do.*

Anyway, this time of year avalanches aren't much of a threat around here, the snow having solidified. Especially in early morning. However, by late afternoon, after the sun has baked the peak, a heavy, slow, wet slide can let loose from a steep slope like this. He'll need to be more cautious on his return.

"Low danger," he says aloud with satisfaction.

As he crosses the couloir, his boots scrape along like he's a ghoul dragging a chain, with billowy white fog-ghosts accompanying him. He'd give a million dollars right now for Korka's and Aron's company. Even verbal jabs from his sister or a sit-down strike from his brother. Being alone is frightening. This is not like when he challenged nature for fun on solo hikes. Not like when he and Mark made up stupid challenges and thought they were superheroes for meeting them.

Back then, he thought he was cool and tough. Thought he was testing himself. Only now, on this journey, does he understand what testing his limits really means, and it's no sport. Too much is riding on his getting to that store, loading up, and getting out before he's recognized. Too much is riding on getting back to his family to feed and protect them. It's up to him to keep them together and to dodge those who would separate them.

Bark breakfast or not, he's so weak and hungry that he can hardly move, and that's terrifying. He has never felt this weak and sluggish. Plus, dragging himself through snow again after weeks of springtime warmth in Leah's sheltered valley is soul crushing.

He's been trying not to think about her, but suddenly there she is in his mind's eye. *Leah. Are you okay? As lonely now as I am?*

He shivers and focuses on putting one boot in front of the other and dropping a chip of bark from his pocket every now and again. *Like Hansel and Gretel's breadcrumb trail, but not edible,* he muses. Another trick he learned from a wilderness-survival manual. This technique was once used by First Nations people, who dropped the bits from their canoes into the water in quiet, foggy inlets. GPS way-point plotting might be more effective and up to date, but you kind of need a GPS for that.

He tries to warm himself with memories of walking this terrain with his father. Both of them being young and strong, and the night's snowstorm having ended, they got to Wolfsburg in a few hours flat. That's when they treated themselves to hot chocolate with peaks of whipped cream in the corner of a general store that was like something out of a time warp.

Resting uses up 70 calories per hour and walking uses 180, one of his survival manuals instructed. Without sufficient protein, a hiker will experience a drop in energy and mental sharpness.

No kidding. When was the last time he had 180 calories? How many calories in a slice of bark, anyway? To kick himself into positive mode, he pictures being served hot chocolate, steak, and French fries in a Wolfsburg café by a cute, friendly waitress who offers him a snowmobile ride back up and over the pass. When he arrives back at the mining village tomorrow, Korka and Aron will fly into his arms, all being forgiven, and the three will live happily in their cabin till his birthday. Mark will show up with a double-fudge birthday cake, and —

In the thickening fog, he trips on a fallen branch, and one foot slides out from under him. A cry escapes his mouth, and suddenly he's hurtling down the steep slope at back-breaking speed. Frantic, he reaches out to catch something, anything, to arrest his fall. The branch he grabs jerks him to an abrupt halt, but the pain that sears through his shoulder makes him yelp like a coyote.

For five minutes he lies in the snow trembling, teeth clenched, fearful of moving. The pain makes it hard to think. Damn the fog and his careless footwork! He knows exactly what he has done: dislocated his right shoulder. As a near-EMT, he also knows there's only one way to deal with it before it swells to the point where he can't do anything for it. It's not like there are any doctors around, and he might get turned in to police if he tries to see one in Wolfsburg, anyway. So, grunting and biting his tongue, he sits up, then stands, cupping the throbbing, useless arm in the opposite hand and holding it away from his body.

Anterior or posterior dislocation? his EMT practice-exam questions demanded. *Clavicle or arm broken, too?*

Jon pushes gently on his clavicle and feels the strange, unround shape of his injured shoulder. Anterior, nothing else broken. Best-case scenario.

He trudges to a massive downed tree and, with his good arm, gathers roughly five kilograms of rocks into his sleeping bag's stuff sack. Next, biting his tongue, he loops the sack's drawstring around the wrist of his injured arm and lies down full length on the log, stomach and forehead touching the bark. Luckily, the log is the right height so that his hand and the bag dangle without touching the snowy ground, and he manages to wriggle until the shoulder is just off the edge of the log.

Slowly, painfully, for more than five minutes, he lets the sack of rocks exert the steady force of gravity on his shoulder, until he hears a clunk and feels a new bolt of pain that indicates the ball of the arm bone has popped back into its shoulder socket.

"Good job!" he reassures himself. "Way to be brave. That should ease the pain." *I must be delirious, talking to myself.* "Now take a few aspirin, swaddle the arm for protection, and put it in a sling. Immobilization is important so you don't reinjure it. I'd say another ten minutes of rest before you get too chilled, and then you can carry on." He'll have to carry his pack on the other shoulder.

It's now a low, dull pain rather than a shrieking, intolerable one. And he got it in time, thanks to his EMT training. He allows himself a moment of pride.

Hours later, still dropping bark chips onto the snow, he shuffles into town and heads straight for the general store. He reminds himself to ask someone there for today's date after he loads up on supplies, since he has lost all track of time. The elderly bearded man at the desk stares at him open-mouthed.

"You jis' roll in from somewhere wild? Fought a grizzly on the way? Look like death warmed over," he says. "What can I do ya for?"

Jon manages to force a smile on his pinched face and rattles off the list so fast that the old-timer raises an eyebrow as thick as his curled moustache. "Camp stove fuel, waterproof matches, nuts, a dozen chocolate bars, oatmeal, water-purification tablets, soup packets, dried fruit, dried milk, and a folding saw if you have one."

The bell on the door jingles. And just as Jon holds out his pack for the man to start filling, a person behind him speaks. "That's quite the pile of supplies, son. Planning to be out in the backcountry a while?"

Jon turns to see a uniformed policeman standing there, looking at him with eyes narrowed, static coming from the radio on his belt. Just his rotten luck.

"How'd you hurt that shoulder? Where've you come in from?"

As casually as he can, he names the national park on the opposite side of town, not the direction from which he actually arrived. He keeps his right arm crooked, so it looks normal, more or less. "I'm headed right back up there. Had a little tumble, but my girlfriend's a nurse, so it's all good. We're enjoying a camping trip as a break from university." He hasn't managed to grow a moustache or beard to disguise himself these past months, but he's got a chaos of peach fuzz and an unruly mop that might make him harder to identify.

"Uh-huh. See any kids on your travels? Search and Rescue is after three young runaways that've been missing for a while. In fact, an officer from Peakton keeps coming here, annoying me plenty, he's so obsessed with finding 'em. Ever since they disappeared, he's been coming every week or two to look for them."

Before Jon can answer, the radio on the policeman's belt crackles and a scratchy message comes in. "Two young people detained at the old mining town," the voice says. "Both suffering smoke inhalation from the fire. Unfortunately, they escaped before we got them loaded into the helicopter. Manhunt on."

"Fire?" Jon manages to choke out. "Manhunt?"

"The old mining town went up in flames last night," the store clerk says, shaking his head. "Shameless vandals. Pyromaniacs. Kids these days!"

The cop ignores both of them as he backs out of the store, talking into his radio in a low voice.

The minute Jon has paid for and loaded up his goods, he projects a cheerful smile at the store guy and says, "Appreciate it."

"You take care, son," the shopkeeper replies, twisting the handles of his moustache between thumb and finger.

The cop has disappeared, so Jon hightails it back to the trail, thankful for the swirl of cloud obscuring him. As he hurries along, he stuffs the most delicious chocolate bar in the universe into his mouth, counting on it to speed-deliver its calories to his shrunken insides. His newly superheavy pack hangs awkwardly on his left shoulder, which is already aching.

"Wait! Young man!" comes a shout through the fog.

It's not Officer Vine. Not yet, anyway. *The old man, or the cop?* Jon wonders. He's not about to stick around long enough to find out.

With a burst of speed, he aims for the trailhead. The farther he gets from the general store, the more the mist wraps itself around him like protective cotton batting. Soon he's climbing, following the bark chips on a trail otherwise totally swallowed by the cloud.

So, kids, what do we do when visibility is bad? asks his father.

Stay put, Jon would once have said with confidence. But now he whispers, "Not when it means getting arrested and not being there for your family."

Good, Jon, his parka-bundled mother says as she hustles along beside him. *But won't your pursuers come after you?*

"No," he mutters. "Because no matter how hard they try, they can't walk in a straight line without a sightline or compass. And they don't know about my bark chips. They'll end up going in a circle, at least for a while."

He has several hours of hiking ahead of him and only one shoulder on which to hang a heavy load. He's determined, but will he have the strength? The radio report weighs on his mind, and it brings an additional risk, that Officer Vine will get wind of his visit to the general store. He tries not to imagine the worst: Korka and Aron on the run and possibly injured, the three of them captured by Officer Vine, the family split up despite their best efforts to stay together.

TWENTY-FOUR

By the time Korka and Aron hear a second helicopter's blades chopping the air overhead, they're well up the trail, above the former mining town, navigating nervously through a thickening fog soup with their compass. They have very little but sleeping gear in the pack Korka wears. Not even the water-purification tablets or folding saw, thanks to Bud and crew.

Korka figures their stolen things are either burned to a crisp or in the hands of the group they saw dashing into the forest at dawn, hiding from the first helicopter as it swooped down on the smoking ruins. She guesses that the fire was reported earlier — the smoke must have been visible far away — but the helicopters had to wait for daylight.

"Wonder if those guys burned down the cabins on purpose or by accident," she says. "Either way, they're in big trouble. But at least it distracts people from looking for us."

"I saw two getting caught by whoever came in the first helicopter," Aron says. "The assholes deserve jail time."

"Language." Korka imitates her mother, smiling.

But her grin gradually fades as they reach snowline. The terrain gets steeper and more slippery, her breath shorter, and the mist thicker. Slogging up a mountain pass in near-zero-visibility conditions, with wild animals that could jump them at any time, is dangerous and a little crazy. Doing so with no saw, flint, or matches for a fire, no headlamps or water purifier — oh my God.

"Gotta make it to the cave before dark," she reminds Aron. "Really must not pass it without knowing," she adds, shivering.

"Jon said watch for an avalanche chute," Aron replies.

"Yeah, he said it runs right over the trail after the three trees where we need to stop."

Aron is lagging, and Korka doesn't have the strength to tug him along, let alone piggyback him. She'd give anything to have Jon with them now, even with his bossy directions and know-it-all personality. Especially with his bossy directions and ... whatever.

"If it weren't for Jon, we'd never have gotten all the way to the mining town," she admits, mumbling half to herself, maybe to keep the two of them alert. "He knew how to look after your blister and your fever and my sprained ankle." Without him, they'd have long since been lost, starved, too injured to continue. "Without Jon —"

"— Officer Vine would have us," comes Aron's quiet voice beside her.

"Or we'd be back in Peakton, separated and put in different homes." Unable to retrieve Aron easily from some facility for the developmentally challenged, even when Jon turned eighteen. She might even be living with Officer Vine, she thinks with a shudder.

She hasn't been an easy person to travel with these past few months, she knows, but she wouldn't trade their threesome for anything, especially not for becoming part of the Vine household. For sure, their parents wouldn't have wanted them split up.

"What's for lunch?" Aron asks.

"Nothing yet," she insists, and tightens her handhold to coax him along.

She flashes back to all the times her father did that for her, encouraged her on when she was exhausted, their hands linked. Her father, so stressed with money problems that he was not thinking straight that day. For the first time it occurs to her that their parents' deaths must have stung Jon the worst of all of them, since he was their helper on the accounting stuff. She wanted to help with the business, but couldn't figure out how to at her age. All she did was twist the knife in Jon the other night, tell him that he should've helped them more. Yet in the face of that cruelty, all he did was hang his head and admit he should have.

"Jon did this slope all by himself yesterday," she reminds her brother. "With hardly any food in his stomach."

"And he left all his gear with us," Aron agrees, straightening his shoulders and stepping up his pace a little.

"He's a strong, brave, and selfless leader," Korka says, wiping a damp cheek with her mitten. "He has only ever wanted to help and protect us. I shouldn't have gotten so mad."

Aron squeezes her hand and pulls *her* onward.

"He can't help being a little strong-minded, given he's the oldest," she continues. "He had to step into Mom's and Dad's shoes without even time to feel awful about their accident. I think he's been blaming himself for it."

Aron halts and looks up at her, a question mark on his face.

"He was their numbers person. Must've known how far in debt the business was. He figured the stress of that distracted them the day they died. He's been carrying that guilt around on him like a pack of rocks all this trip." She sniffs, fighting back tears.

She sighs and continues. "Maybe I could've offered to drop my Krav Maga classes before Dad had to tell me to. Maybe I could've gotten babysitting jobs, or refused allowance. I just didn't know. I miss them so badly." Tears are splashing on the snow underfoot. She knows she shouldn't cry in front of Aron, should stay strong for him, but she can't help it.

"It's okay," Aron says, his own water-filled eyes gazing up at her.

She has craved her parents' reassuring presence every minute of this march. Their hands clasping hers; their laughter; their way of turning long, hard hikes into fun with snowball fights and Viking legend tales. Their ever-present courage and amazing energy.

"Remember how Mom would use her hands to do puppet shadows by candlelight in the tent?" Korka asks.

"Uh-huh."

They loved life, they loved each other, and they loved their children.

Yet, if they'd felt forced to close the business and do something else, Korka knows all too well she'd have objected with all the kicking and screaming her spoiled self tended to do. No more of that, she vows now. Time to grow up. She has been so busy dissing Jon for not being a team player, she hasn't been working hard enough on being a better one herself.

"I'm only fourteen," she says with a gulp. And now totally responsible for keeping herself and Aron alive. It's scary, and she can't believe she ever wished for it. Only now can she understand how overwhelming it was for Jon to have been thrust suddenly into his role as their protector, unable to relax or show fear. "What if someone turns Jon in when he reaches Wolfsburg? What if he slips and falls, or faints on the way there, and freezes to death in the snow, all alone with no one to help him?"

"Stop worrying, Korka. Let's just get to the cave," Aron pleads.

Right now, putting one foot in front of another, all she can do is fantasize they'll meet Jon coming in the other direction. Not just because they desperately need everything he's bringing from the store, but because all three of them would drop their packs and race through the fog and join together for the wildest, greatest reunion ever. And no one would worry about petty little arguments of the past.

After all, they're a family, and despite everything that has happened, she's proud of them for sticking together as much as they have, for keeping each other alive.

But she doesn't see Jon approaching in the fog. He can't possibly get to town and back up here before tonight or tomorrow, she reminds herself. And with an emaciated body, even that would be a superman achievement.

"Lunch?" Aron asks again.

"You know exactly what's for lunch, thief." With effort, Korka pulls herself together and grins. "Raw hot dogs."

"Wrong. Cooked hot dogs. I know how to start a fire without matches or flint."

"That's true," she says. "Cooked hot dogs, boiled snow, and some warmth and protection in the cave would be fine with me. But step it up, partner, so we get there before dark."

When Aron pushes his damp glove into hers and picks up his pace with brave effort, she pats his head the same way Jon does, and says, "Carry on, Young Viking. We're nearly at that cave." Given how far they've trekked already and the way the snowy ground is levelling out, she hopes they are indeed near the top of the pass.

"Dad was the one who showed Jon the cave, you know," she says. "So, it'll be cozy and safe and not hard to find. Maybe Dad's spirit will be there to greet us and protect us and tell us stories. If not, we can do that together, because we learned from the best, eh? Plus, I can't wait for you to show me how to start a fire in the damp without matches or flint."

Not that she couldn't start a fire herself if she had to. She knows how to use a hand drill, rotating a stick between her hands vigorously to light tinder. But her little brother is way better at the difficult task, and he needs to feel needed, equal, and independent — all the stuff she's been wishing Jon would make her feel. And that's something she can help him with, if she puts her mind to it.

"Three trees growing from one trunk!" Aron shouts.

And there they are, to the right, three alpine firs thrusting out of the fog.

"You got it," she says.

"*We* got it," he corrects her, and they hug — a long, triumphant, relieved hug. Then they turn right and slog upward, firmly following in Jon's still-visible boot prints from yesterday.

Amazingly, Aron doesn't hesitate at the dark, narrow entrance. He removes his pack, crawls just inside, and then turns, head poking out, to pull the pack in after him. He reaches out to help her in.

Then he pulls treasures out of his pocket that she didn't know he had: fungus from the mining village, moss, and tiny twigs — all excellent fire starters.

"The twigs are from a bird's nest," he boasts, eyes sparkling.

"The best kind of wood kindling," she says.

As she crawls out of the cave on her way to gather larger sticks and to stuff their stainless-steel water bottles with snow, she looks back at her little brother. He is creating his hand drill like an expert. *Good job, Young Viking.*

TWENTY-FIVE

Despite having stuffed down two chocolate bars and some salmon jerky, or maybe because of eating that weird combo so quickly while huffing up a steep slope, Jon is feeling hampered by a stomach ache. He's also kicking himself for forgetting to ask the storekeeper the date.

Worse, he keeps imagining the sound of boots right behind him. And the pack rubs where the strap pulls heavily on his one good shoulder. The other shoulder is throbbing, and the aspirin he took only seems to make him sleepy.

Maybe he can step off the trail and climb into his sleeping bag for a few hours? No! Korka and Aron somehow survived their cabin burning down and narrowly escaped being taken away by officials. That could mean they're injured or without gear, and being chased. What happened? Did they start a campfire too close to the shack? Surely, they wouldn't have tried lighting a fire in the unusable pot-bellied stove.

Or did someone else show up at the site and start a campfire that spread? Maybe the two youths on the run aren't Korka and Aron. Maybe instead, his siblings are hiding in the woods, having escaped just in time from party pyromaniacs.

Whatever the case, they need him. He must keep going, keep pressing forward. *I am not tired*, he tells himself.

He wishes Korka and Aron were here to encourage him. Even a wary Aron and a bratty Korka. No! She's not bratty, just a normal teenager, desperate to be accepted for the strong, independent girl she is. A girl not unlike Leah.

"Too good for me?" Leah demanded when he chickened out of kissing her. "Or is it that you can't control me, like you do poor Korka and Aron? You're overprotecting them, Jon. And driving them away in the process. You want to drive me away, too?"

He kicks a lump of snow on the trail. Without meaning to, he has driven away all three of them. But if he's controlling it's 'cause he got dumped into the deep end, having to look after two kids for these months, and he's doing it the hard way: on the move, in hiding, in the backcountry.

Okay, so maybe he's learned a lesson or two. Give Korka more independence. She's the most competent fourteen-year-old he knows. And outspoken, which you'd have to be to rise to the situation he's put them in. Scratch that. The situation the three voted themselves into.

He hears his father's voice: *In a forest, trees grow toward the sky, reaching for whatever light they can get. Some tree species have a "leader" that keeps that role by chemically suppressing side branches from reaching higher.*

Is that him? Has he been suppressing them? Yes! The disastrous snow cave incident when they were all young was his first taste of shepherding them on an adventure, one that went bad and could've gone way worse. Ever since then, he's been overprotecting them, as if that could ease his guilt and prevent future disaster. A pointless five-year guilt trip, according to Aron. Jon was only twelve then, after all.

The snow cave collapse was not his fault, and choosing not to speak much is not a weakness, Aron assured him. "It's just me," he said. Korka, too, is a strong sapling fighting for sunlight to shoot to the skies. He has been standing in their daylight.

Trauma can turn a single tree into one that shares its trunk with others. Beavers, flooding, or fire temporarily stop growth.

Beavers, flooding, fire — or an avalanche that devastates the family.

And then the tree suddenly rebounds with a twin.

Or triplets.

His thoughts may be random, but they're keeping him awake and moving forward.

Important things come in threes. Faith, hope, and love. Truth, courage, and compassion. Harmony, wisdom, and understanding. And the fearless Gunnarsson kids.

If you're still alive and well and uncaught, Korka and Aron, I'm coming to get you, Jon vows. *No matter what it takes, physically or mentally. I've been training all my life for this test. The other tests may have been about me. This one's not.*

One arm in a sling, hurting all over, and depleted of energy, he wills his lungs to take one more breath and his boots to take one more step. And then another. Gritting his teeth, he shoves everything out of his mind but an image of Korka and Aron huddled near the mining town, all equipment gone, officers and drunk hikers both searching for them.

No, that's the wrong picture, he tells himself. They escaped the fire, and they know how to survive even if every item they own has been stolen or charred. They know how to dodge pursuers, even in a heavy fog, and they're brave and stoic enough to sit tight somewhere safe till he reaches them. They've got what it takes to survive, even if he fails them, he admits for once. What they didn't know before this journey, they've learned on it. *A strong leader creates other leaders.*

He halts, unsure why. Was it a noise behind him, or something different in the terrain? He has outclimbed the fog, and there's a snowy gully ahead. He thinks about the couloir he crossed early this morning. How much sun has the peak absorbed since then? Enough to create the conditions for a late-season slide?

He sits down and rolls out of his pack, then digs his one free hand into the bone-chilling white stuff to make a snow pit. Without a saw, his whole body pounding in pain, and his mind ready to collapse, it's not easy to chop out a study block. But when he succeeds, he taps on it till it fractures. "Moderate danger between here and the cave," he mutters.

He tries to struggle up, but to his shock and horror, he can't. It's like the snowy ground has an overwhelming magnetic hold on him, and his knees have caved in. Worse, even the uninjured shoulder refuses to accept the load of the pack anymore. He closes his eyes, counts to ten, and … the world whirls dizzyingly fast. Nothing exists but a desire to sleep.

That would mean death, admonishes his father. *Hypothermia is setting in already, because there's no fat on your bones. Ditch some weight in your pack and get to your brother and sister, now. Take the risk of the crossing. You'll be okay.*

Jon raises his head and forces both hands to dig into the pack to remove nonessentials. The hands like it in there. It's warmer. They want to stay. Eventually, he tosses a few things out, then forgets what he's doing and crawls forward, one-handed, into the avalanche zone. A strap of his half-empty pack is tangled loosely around his ankle. The contents of his pack dribble out till the pack falls off his ankle and gets left behind. He's on one hand and two knees, shivering, eyes half-closed. Each time he drags a knee forward, it feels like a major accomplishment, though by now he has lost all sense of time or reason.

He knows nothing except that he must cross the gully. He must make it to the other side before snow slides out of the mountainside above like a waterfall and takes him, as it took his parents, in a cold, white death spin.

He hears the *whumpf* above and knows it's too late, that his body may never be found, that Korka and Aron will have yet another funeral to plan and pay for, another guardian to grieve. He did his best. He tried, he tried so hard, but this is his worst nightmare — failing them.

His mind is whirling, whirling, and he feels dizziness overtake him, numbness embrace him. In one last act, he raises his tin whistle to his lips and blows the longest, hardest, shrillest blast he can.

TWENTY-SIX

How much later he'll never know, he becomes aware of
shouting in the distance and stirs. "Jon?" someone is bellowing.

Officer Vine.

His first thought: He's been caught. Months of hunger,
danger, and tension — all for nothing.

Jon opens his eyes and looks about. Trees are waving
in the breeze overhead. There's no fog. It's late afternoon,
shadows falling already. He's sprawled in the snow on
the mining village side of the avalanche chute, beside the
three-tree feature. There was no snow slide on his way
across, no avalanche that took him. It was a hallucination,

a nightmare. He manages to turn his head to look behind him. The pack lies abandoned in the middle of the couloir, its contents strewn all the way to the far side. What happened? Why did he leave his pack and its precious contents behind? Because he couldn't walk, he remembers. Couldn't pull the whole backpack even by crawling. He was done for.

"Jon?" It's Officer Vine hollering again, from the Wolfsburg side of the avalanche zone. He seems to have paused there, like he's afraid to cross.

"I'm here," Jon calls out, half-inclined to surrender and half-determined to taunt his adversary.

"I'm coming across," Officer Vine shouts.

"No!" Jon struggles to a sitting position. "It's not safe! Extreme danger! The snow's about to give way!"

"Liar. Why would you have crossed, then?"

But Jon hears hesitation in the officer's voice. The speculation of even a young, weakened Gunnarsson is worthy of respect. For a few minutes, then, there's silence, Officer Vine holding his ground, not trotting over. Good. While there's still distance between them, there's a chance of escaping his clutches.

"Do you have Korka and Aron?" Jon finally calls over, a tremor in his voice.

"What? They're not with you, Jon? You've lost them? Are they alive?" Then the worry in his voice is replaced by anger. "You should never have left home. I offered you shelter and family out of the kindness of my heart, yet you decided to risk the lives of your brother and sister, and numerous Search and Rescue personnel, as well."

Jon focuses on the blurred figure across the chute. He sees no one with him. "You wanted to separate us. You wanted to send Aron to a home."

The officer shakes his head. "I wanted to help your family. I'm disappointed you took off instead. Tell me when your brother and sister were last with you, and where."

"Why would I?"

"My home and my offer remain open, despite your stubbornness, Jon. As your father's long-time acquaintance, I can assure you this is not what he or your mother would have wanted to see happen."

"We don't need anyone, Officer Vine!"

"I know you think you don't, but there are the legalities, Jon. At least tell me where you think your siblings are. Please tell me they're still alive. Korka, the sparky one, and Aron, who must be terrified."

"Sparky? Korka? That's 'cause she's smart and capable. No one gives her the respect she deserves. It took me a while to figure that out, but I'd trust my life to her. I'm proud to have her as my sister." Jon's own fury fuels his words. "As for Aron, he's far from terrified. If it weren't for him and his amazing instincts, the three of us wouldn't still be around. He damn near saved my mother's and father's lives, too. He's more tuned into the outdoors than all the Search and Rescue professionals put together. He's —"

"The kid who doesn't talk and thinks he's a Viking?"

Jon, shaking with anger, finally manages to rise and take three wobbly steps forward. "We're a team. A threesome. We survived because —"

"— we learned to work together," comes Korka's voice.

"We know survival skills," Aron says.

Relief overwhelms Jon as he whirls around and staggers over to them, both standing tall, their single pack on the ground between them. "You w-w-were in the cave. You heard my whistle."

Korka and Aron nod, and the three of them direct withering looks at the policeman, whose jaw has dropped.

"I can speak when I want," Aron informs him, eyes flashing across the expanse of snow. "And I know who to trust."

"I'm coming over to apprehend all three of you," Officer Vine shouts.

The roar of a snowmobile engine behind him drowns out whatever else he might have said. Jon's aching shoulders hunch as he spots the uniform of a Search and Rescue member driving, a passenger behind him. The passenger climbs off, a figure vaguely familiar even in helmet and snowmobile suit.

"That's them!" Officer Vine tells the driver. "He claims the chute isn't stable, but only because he doesn't want to be caught."

The man nods, grabs a shovel from the back of his machine, and constructs a snow pit so quickly that Jon raises an eyebrow. But he also feels his heart sinking.

"Moderate danger. Doable," the man declares. "Son, I'm Murray Pierce from County Search and Rescue. I'm going to cross over with avalanche beacons for each one of you. Stay right where you are."

"Not a chance," Jon retorts, taking Korka and Aron by the hands and stepping back in a futile show of bravery.

"You're in no condition to run," Officer Vine yells. "And you don't want to be resisting arrest, do you?"

"Greg," says the passenger. A woman's voice. "You can't arrest them." She removes her helmet and shakes long dark hair out of her face.

Jon, Korka, and Aron stand open-mouthed, staring at Amanda Pierce, their social worker. "What are you doing here?" Jon demands, unsure whose side she's on.

"Murray is my brother," she says with a quick, businesslike smile. "When I heard a report of the mining village burning down, I drove to his house in Wolfsburg, intending to hike in with him to see if I could help. Then Murray got the message from Officer Vine that you, Jon, were on the pass, alone. I was so worried about the three of you, I insisted on riding up with him."

"We're fine," Korka says, taking two steps forward. She hesitates as she glances up the chute.

"Do you know what day it is?" Amanda asks, grabbing the beacons from her brother's hand and fearlessly walking across the gully till she's facing them from a few steps away. The late-afternoon sun shines brightly on her welcoming face.

Her brother follows. Officer Vine stays glued to his side of the couloir.

"A Sunday," Aron guesses. "There was a party in the ghost town yesterday."

"An anniversary of our parents' death?" Korka asks, choked up.

"We've lost all track of time," Jon admits. Their goal was his birthday, and he doesn't even know what the date is. His exhaustion is returning, his entire body swaying with the effort of standing.

"It's May eleventh," she says. "A few days past your birthday, Jon."

"I'm eighteen," he says weakly.

"You're eighteen!" Korka and Aron shout as the implication dawns on them.

Amanda, wearing the boots that resemble their mother's, takes Jon's good arm to support him. Her brother steadies him from the other side. Jon doesn't flinch or resist as the two place a beacon around his neck, then around Korka's and Aron's, and lead the siblings in a human chain across to the snowmobile. Amanda and her brother offer respectful glances to Jon as he pushes one boot ahead of the other.

Korka and Aron bend down at intervals to scoop up the spilled gear along the way, and when they reach Jon's abandoned backpack, they stuff these items into it. When they reach the far side, they dive for some chocolate bars in the snow, unwrap them, and bite into them like starved soldiers on rations.

Officer Vine's face is stony, his eyes narrowed at Amanda. Amanda's tall brother leans against the snowmobile.

"You won't get away scot-free," Officer Vine tells the Gunnarssons. "You've caused way too much trouble for me to just let this be. But," he adds grudgingly, "I'm glad you're alive."

"Trouble?" Korka says. "We're three kids who lost both our parents and went on a camping trip to deal with it in our own way. How is that illegal?"

"Jon," Amanda says, "hop on behind Murray. The truck and trailer for the snowmobile aren't far away, just down at snowline. Murray can get you settled in the truck and return for us. Officer Vine and I can walk with Korka and Aron till Murray gets back, if they're up for it."

"Up for it," Korka declares, and Aron gives a thumbs-up.

"Did you catch Bud and the other seven losers who started the fire?" Korka asks Officer Vine.

He pats the radio on his belt. "Yes, we did. Sounds like we'll need a statement from you."

Jon wants to ask Korka about the fire and their trek up here, but he's spent and filled with a jumble of emotions. Relieved at seeing his brother and sister alive. Happy, and at the same time humiliated, to be rescued. Also wondering where Leah is and whether she's okay.

TWENTY-SEVEN

After a few days recuperating at Amanda's brother's house in Wolfsburg, and being tended to by a doctor there, the family returns to Peakton together. Jon feels dumbstruck at the weirdness of sitting at a café table with his siblings and Amanda, ordering from a menu with hamburgers and French fries on it.

They're still endlessly hungry, yes, but mostly what they all feel today, he figures, is dog-tired, homeless, penniless, and sad. It's particularly bizarre to look across the grassy park and see their former rental house, where strangers are moving about as if they live there — and to realize those strangers *do* live there. It should be their parents at the door, eager to welcome them home.

"Your things were moved to the garage, then to a storage facility," Amanda informs them gently.

"Where will we live?" Aron asks, looking up at Jon.

"We'll find a basement suite or something," he says. "I'll get a full-time job —"

"— after you graduate from high school," Amanda inserts sternly.

"Of course." There's still a month and a half of the school year left, so it's possible he could graduate on the normal schedule. If not, it'll just require some online classes.

"I'll mow lawns or shovel snow after school," Aron offers.

Korka speaks up. "I'll babysit." She pauses. "Wait! Basement suite! Amanda, can I borrow your phone?"

Amanda hands it over with a smile. Korka leaps up and moves away, and they all stare after her.

"Jon!" comes a voice from the café doorway. As Mark bounds over to the table, Jon rises with a wide grin. Mark gives bear hugs to Jon and Aron. "You made it home without a single emergency phone call to me," he says. "Not that I expected for a minute you'd need one. Hi, Amanda, heard all about you. I'm Mark."

Amanda shakes his outstretched hand. "Nice to meet you, Mark. Sit down and join us."

"Hmm, Big Viking, you look like you just ran an ultramarathon after fasting. Gotta fatten you up, clearly. Happy birthday, by the way. Now we can go out drinking, eh? Aron, you looked after your crazy big brother, did you? And I bet Korka kicked ass a few times." He pauses and looks around at them. "What's happening now you're back?"

"We were just discussing that," Amanda says.

Amanda seems hesitant, but Jon says, "Mark can stay and listen in. He's like family."

"Okay. Well, your parents' debts were paid off by the estate once the life insurance came through. Remaining funds have been divided into three accounts, yours available immediately and Korka's and Aron's locked in a trust fund till they turn eighteen. There's enough for you to live off for a little while, but yes, it would be wise to start working as soon as you can."

"She means get that EMT qualification sooner rather than later," Mark says.

"EMT?" Amanda asks, raising an eyebrow.

"I've been studying for it for a long time. I could train right after I finish high school," Jon informs her. For the first time since their parents died, he feels a spark of excitement about the future. "And be qualified in eleven weeks."

"So, you're not going to try and revive your parents' school?"

Jon shakes his head, and Aron nods in agreement.

Korka, who has just walked back to their table, says, "No way. We'll get some money from the equipment, maybe. But Jon's going to be the best EMT Peakton ever had, and I'm going to teach Krav Maga to little kids."

"You are?" Jon asks, smiling approvingly, not at all surprised at his sister's confidence.

"That, and clean Mrs. Alpern's basement Krav Maga studio every day after school, in return for us three living in two of the three storage rooms next to it. We just have to reorganize the storage spaces. There's a bathroom and kitchenette in the basement, too. I just arranged all that with Mrs. Alpern, and we just need Amanda to approve it." Her face is pink, and she's breathless with excitement.

"I'm likely to approve it," Amanda says with a smile.

Aron gives Korka a thumbs-up. Which means, Jon figures, that Mrs. Alpern is okay.

"You sure know how to make things happen, Korka," Mark comments. "So, all three of you are going to live in two little rooms?"

They laugh.

"More spacious than our green tent," Korka says.

"Want me to help you move your stuff from storage to there?" Mark asks.

"Maybe tomorrow," Jon replies with a yawn. "We'd better see it first. We're used to not having much stuff, anyway, and we're kind of low on energy right now."

"Okay."

"Join us to eat, Mark?" Amanda suggests as plates loaded with food arrive. "It's on me."

"You bet! Thanks!" He orders a burger and salad.

"Appreciate all you've done, Amanda," Jon says soberly. "I can't believe we lasted almost three months, and that it's all working out. All except for having made an enemy of Officer Vine, maybe."

"Not so much," she says. "He's over it already, boasting

to everyone that he found you emaciated and without a thing left in your backpack."

"Technically true," Jon allows.

"He's also telling everyone you were brave and smart to have emerged alive, and that all three of you are chips off the old block."

Jon winks at Korka and Aron, who smile back.

Across the park, he spies the new renters backing a fancy car out of what used to be *their* garage, and he grimaces. The garage is absolutely empty, scrubbed clean and repainted white, not like when they lived there and it sported peeling blue paint, shelves sagging with outdoor gear, and a locker full of camping food.

He studies the plate of food in front of him, appetite disappearing. Their lives have changed drastically, and it's going to take a lot to get used to being "home" in such different circumstances.

"It's okay," Amanda whispers, like she has read his mind. "It won't be easy, but you're the most resilient family I've ever met." She sounds like she means it.

"Thanks," he says.

A thin, middle-aged woman with a brown shawl over her shoulders enters the café and approaches the group hesitantly.

"Are you the Gunnarssons?"

"Yup," Jon replies, certain he has never seen her before.

"I'm Sarah Green, and Officer Vine told me I might find you over here. My ex-husband contacted your parents a few months ago about tracking down my daughter, Leah Green. I'm so sorry about your mother and father," she adds quickly, fiddling with her shawl's fringe and casting her eyes to the floor — eyes that bear a startling resemblance to Leah's, Jon notes, his pulse quickening.

"Yeah?" Korka says.

"Do sit down," Amanda offers, but not without first eyeing Jon, Korka, and Aron.

Jon feels his body tense.

"Officer Vine ran into Leah when he was searching for you and contacted me, but he couldn't remember the exact place she'd been camping. He told me to check with you in case you ran across her and have some idea. I don't know if you're still interested in tracking her down. I would pay you, obviously. She's still missing, and I, well, I don't know how to find her."

"Is that the good-looking redhead you told me about?" Mark asks, then winces as Jon kicks him under the table.

"We wouldn't have a clue," Jon says a little too quickly.

"Are you a hiker?" Aron asks the mother.

"Aron," Korka says warningly. They absolutely promised Leah that they wouldn't tell anyone where she was.

"Well, I used to be. Not like Leah. She's amazing since she took your parents' course." Her face brightens for a split second. "But —"

She lowers her head, and Jon fears she's going to cry.

"Did you say your ex-husband?" Jon asks in a softer tone.

"Yes, her stepfather. He's the one who made the original inquiry, but they didn't get along, and ... well, I know she left because of him. Now that I'm alone, I think about her all the time, and I, well, I need her. At least, I need to know if she's okay, and she needs to know she can come home if she wants to. Do you think she's all right? If you lasted all that time in the mountains, she could, too, right? Even though she's alone?"

"I'm sure she's alive and well, but probably lonely," Jon says quietly. Amanda raises an eyebrow. "If she wants to be found, she will be. Can I mark on a map where you might try?"

"Jon!" Korka and Aron exclaim at the same time. Then they go quiet, seeming to hand the decision to him.

Amanda looks from the three to the mother, and a glint of a smile appears. She pulls a park map from her purple briefcase and hands it to Jon.

"I have lots of maps," she says. "You can keep this one, Mrs. Green."

"Oh, thank you," the mother says. "Did you come across her, then?"

Ignoring the question, Jon scribbles on the map in pencil, then pushes it into the mother's hands. "Good luck," he says, looking away from the tears on her face. "Tell her to visit Peakton sometime," he adds.

"I will, I will," Mrs. Green says, pulling her shawl tightly around her tall, slight form. "You're the youngest, right?" she asks Aron. "So, it's not true that you don't speak."

"I speak when I want," Aron replies, pulling himself up tall.

In fact, Aron is taller than when they left town, Jon notices. Maybe they've all grown, despite their weird diet the past few months.

"I see. Well, I'll let you know if I find her," she says hopefully.

A few hours later they marvel over being able to draw money out of a bank machine with a card that Amanda has handed Jon. They buy essentials at the local supermarket, where they receive loud welcome-home greetings and a dozen crushing hugs, like heroes returned from a warzone.

That night, they crash on the shiny tiled floor of one of Mrs. Alpern's emptied basement storage rooms, tucked into their sleeping bags and curled up on their camping pads. Their few possessions are stacked in the corner.

"Did you remember to dig the toilet hole?" Korka kids Jon.

"I didn't see you get firewood or do dishes," he shoots back.

"Aron, you're out of a job starting the campfire," Korka says.

"Yeah, well, hurray that Jon's not the cook anymore," Aron says in an upbeat voice.

It goes quiet in their basement room. It's tight for three people, Jon thinks, and will be even more so when they pull mattresses in tomorrow. But crowded quarters don't bother him, and he doubts it bothers the others for now. And once they clear out the second room, it will seem like a palace compared to their recent living conditions.

"The Norsemen, though still suffering from their losses, are no longer besieged," Aron says into the darkness.

"They've returned home in triumph with many runes of wisdom."

"That makes absolutely no sense," says Korka.

"Vassals clamour for tales of their legendary journey," he continues, "but they keep some secrets to themselves. Meanwhile, in the primeval forest remains a maiden, who will shortly sojourn forth to complete her own saga."

"Oh, shut up," Korka says. Then she giggles. "Who hung the food bag?"

"I don't hear any frogs or crickets or tumbling water," Jon mumbles sleepily.

"Or hooting owls," Aron says, adding, "I miss them."

TWENTY-EIGHT

Crisp leaves are falling through the September air, some evergreen branches have turned a brilliant bronze, and the cantaloupe-coloured sun is sinking behind the mountains. Jon's digging the toilet hole. Aron's starting the fire, and Korka is whipping up something that smells like a mouth-watering curry.

Jon's not coaching or critiquing them anymore. It feels natural this way. It feels totally okay.

Mark is staking his tent beside theirs.

"Add the onions now," Leah directs Korka, "not a minute later. And when it's ready to serve, use this pan to start the Dutch-oven upside-down peach cake."

"Dutch-oven peach cake! No way! I'm disappearing into the woods right now to find *me* a peach-cake maker," Mark exclaims, elbowing Jon, which makes Jon smile.

"Jon never used to trust us around the food in case we snuck some," Korka says.

"We didn't have much to sneak once the ravens visited," Aron adds.

"Yeah, that was bad luck, but it's probably why we joined up with Leah for as long as we did," Jon reminds them. "It's hard to admit, but you were always better than us at getting and cooking food, Leah."

"Of course it's hard to admit," she says, "but you managed it just now, for which I salute you!"

"I guess it's why your campfire cooking courses in Peakton are getting so many sign-ups," Jon continues admiringly. He can hardly believe that after returning from the woods, she and her mother moved to Peakton and started up outdoor-survival courses, filling the niche his parents had left, buying the business's equipment from the Gunnarsson kids, and restarting a business he and his siblings didn't want to take over.

Leah confided to him that she's going to counselling, which seems to be helping her face her issues. She appears more optimistic now, less on guard against the world. She never mentions her former stepfather, nor does her mother.

"Thanks. My mom's been a big help, and we appreciate your marketing and accounting skills, Jon," Leah says. "We also couldn't do without Mark buying supplies, muscling them around, and shuttle driving. Now that you've got your EMT certification, maybe you can even drop in as a guest teacher once in a while." She pushes her red hair over her shoulders and gives Jon a glowing smile.

Jon smiles back, feeling his face grow warm.

"Like Aron with his fire-starting lessons," Leah continues. "People flock to them. They think he's some kind of genius."

"I am." Aron grins as he peeks into the pot on the camp stove.

"Ho! Listen to the modesty!" Mark exclaims.

"What's your most popular class?" Jon asks Leah, though he already suspects which one.

Leah grins. "Building hidden bunkers."

"But is that actually outdoor survival?" Korka asks. "Our parents never taught anything like it. I thought that sort of course was for paranoid wackos."

"It helped you survive," Leah says quietly. "And thrive," she adds. "If you want, Korka, you could help me with the cooking classes."

"No!" Mark says, laughing. "I prefer your cooking, Leah."

"Ha!" Korka responds. "Mark's right just this once. I'm nowhere near good enough, but thanks, anyway. Plus, grade ten turns out to have a lot of homework, which is tough on top of teaching the kiddies for Mrs. Alpern and doing as much babysitting as I can fit in. But we're earning enough to move into a real apartment soon. Right, Jon?"

"You got it, boss."

"Worth celebrating!" Mark says, handing bottles of beer to Jon and Leah.

"What about me?" Korka says slyly.

"A couple more years, kiddo," Mark responds, patting her on the head.

She swipes him gently with her leg, almost toppling his open bottle into the dirt.

He laughs. "Easy there, Lady Viking!"

"You're all amazingly busy," Leah says. "It's a miracle we managed to pull off a camping trip this weekend."

"Been a long time," Jon admits. He leans back, hands behind his head, relaxing for the first time in weeks.

"Curry's ready!" Korka announces a few minutes later, prompting everyone to wash their hands in a basin and move to the log seat, while Aron passes out tin plates and cutlery. "Complete with forest mushrooms I just picked."

"Oh no!" Jon says. "No doubt they spent fifteen minutes in your mouth before you added them?"

"At least. More importantly, Leah approved them."

Aron taste-tests the first spoonful of curry and rice and gives it a thumbs-up. "Way better than hare!"

"Even better than the chocolate bar I found in the snow the day Jon collapsed!" Korka says.

"Almost better than the blueberries I found in the ghost town that morning!" says Aron.

"*Almost?*" says Korka with mock indignation.

During the meal, the air is filled with laughter and teasing. But near the end, Mark speaks up, his voice suddenly sober. "You know, your mom and dad would be really proud of you three."

Leah nods vigorously in agreement.

Jon, his heart aching, smiles at his sister and brother. "They would be."

"The Big Viking got us through it all," says Aron.

"We did it together," says Jon, reaching over to ruffle his brother's hair. "Right, Korka?"

Korka clears her throat. "You know what?" she says.

Everyone looks at her expectantly.

She grins. "It's the guys' turn to wash dishes."

ACKNOWLEDGEMENTS

The region through which the Gunnarssons travel is based roughly on the Willmore Wilderness Park of west-central Alberta, although I fictionalized town names. Thanks above all to John Hammer of Grande Cache, Alberta, member of the Alberta Hunter Education Instructors' Association as well as a school principal. Also to Rob Kaye, long-time national park warden in the area and author of *Born to the Wild*. He did all the math on how much the three could, and needed to, carry. He chose elevations and "supervised" the moose and elk kills. From him I learned the difference between predator and scavenger (look it up yourself) and how long pemmican lasts. He said this of the scene where they stole moose meat from wolves: "I like it. Most people wouldn't believe that three kids could do this. But using burning sticks helps, and having a seventeen-year-old helps. I wouldn't encourage small kids to try this, though."

Warm thanks to all the Dundurn Press team, especially Susan Fitzgerald, Scott Fraser, and Kathryn Lane, but also Sara, Julie, Russell, Elena, Jenny, Melissa, Rudi, Laura, Sophie, Lisa Marie, Ankit, Heather, Kendra, Maria, and Kayleigh.

Special thanks to my valued friend and an inspirational social worker, Laraine Michaelson; Gavin Kennedy (avalanche expert and EMT); and Letitia Sears (lawyer who advised on wills, etc.). A shout-out to writing-retreat leader and author Ellen Schwartz and fellow participants of a Children's Writers and Illustrators of B.C. event on Mayne Island. Thanks, of course, to my husband, Steve Withers, and my editor, Allyson Latta; teen editor, Mal Williams; reader, Jake Seaman; literary agent, Amy Tompkins; Melkorka Hegadóttir, my in-law from Iceland; blog articles at mec.ca; and excellent advice at momgoescamping.com.

I'd like to acknowledge the following books: *Nature Is Your Guide* by Harold Gatty, *Living Off the Land* by Chris McNab, *Extreme Wilderness Survival* by Craig Caudill, *St. John Ambulance Official Wilderness First Aid Guide* by Wayne Merry, *The Lost Ways* by Claude Davis, and *Born to the Wild* by Rob Kaye.

And finally, if you check out the *Mountain Runaways* book trailer at pamwithers.com/book-trailers, you'll appreciate the photography of Lexa Bergen and the models for Jon, Korka, and Aron: Hudson Bergen, Maddie Lehman, and Ryder Magee.

ABOUT THE AUTHOR

Award-winning author Pam Withers has written numerous bestselling outdoor adventure novels for teens. She is also a popular presenter in schools, libraries, and at writers' and educators' conferences. Pam has worked as a journalist, magazine editor, book editor, and associate publisher. She discovered whitewater kayaking in college and pursued slalom kayak racing for many years, and has also spent time as a whitewater kayak instructor, whitewater raft guide, and teen summer-camp coordinator. Pam continues to enjoy time in the outdoors when not writing or indulging in her latest passion, table tennis. She divides her time between Vancouver and the Gulf Islands, British Columbia.